The Songstress

April Simmons

DEDICATION

This book is dedicated to Casey Spradling.

You were gone too soon and you are missed by many.

An oscillating fan turns and turns
And I wait for the breeze to come back to me
But it's never enough to dry the sweat
I'm suffocating but I work diligently
I decorate my room with red plastic gas cans
I won't give up waiting for you…
To pick me up in the shed
For the gathering of the drowning caribou

- *From The Gathering of the Drowning Caribou*
  By April Simmons

CONTENTS

ACKNOWLEDGMENTS

Thanks to my supportive husband, James. Without him, I'd have given up on this project long ago.

Thanks to my sister, Sabrina Hawkins, and my niece, Nancy McLarty, who have loved and supported me despite the crazy.

Thanks to my best friend, Brandy Williams, for being there all the times I needed her.

Thank you to my father, Paul Hawkins, for the support.

Thanks to all my friends for reading during the various draft stages and giving their thoughts.

A big thank you to Megan Ratts for helping out with the dubious editing task. Also thank you to Paul Gann for creating the beautiful cover image.

And thanks to the real Graham.

1 LET GO

I tuned him out after he said I was being let go.

Raphael Strattone and I had a romantic history that went back several years.

When I was just out of high school, I moved to the town of Kilgrave, Maine on a whim. I'd gotten a brochure in the mail about the town and I had fallen in love instantly.

Raphe hired me as a lounge singer at his club back when I was the new girl in town. He acted like this was a huge charity, but he really hired me because he wanted me. He wanted me bad. At first I was wary, but his charm got the best of me and we dated.

Needless to say, things had gone awry.

He fired me a week after I broke up with him. I knew that it was a risk, but one I'd felt the need to take. I couldn't bear his temper or his constant dalliances with a smile anymore. I'd miss the sex. He was great in bed, but that isn't enough sometimes.

Raphe was a tall, lanky half-Italian with a charm that was unbeatable. Unfortunately, he used that charm on everyone.

Marching into the future, I stepped into the first shop with a "NOW HIRING" sign, a tiny convenience store only three blocks from my apartment. I needed some kind of income right away or I'd be homeless. I smiled at the clerk and batted my eyelashes at him.

"Darling, I saw the sign out front...I know it's late, but is there anyone here I can talk to?" The pimple-faced teen glared at me. "I'm the assistant manager. You'll have to come see Maurice during the day. He'll be in tomorrow." He reached under the counter and pulled out an application. "Fill this out and bring it back with you. He'll be here from 8 to 6." As he handed it to me, he focused on my chest. I felt as though he was undressing me with his eyes. I shuddered slightly. I was going to need a shower to wash off the feeling of disgust that crept into my gut.

I thanked him and stepped back into the chilly September night. I wasn't used to the cold. I was a southern girl who'd grown up in Alabama and Georgia. I still hadn't quite adjusted to the New England climate.

I walked home. I found Kal waiting outside of my apartment. Kal was the bouncer at Smoke & Mirrors, Raphe's club.

Kal was a large framed bald man with a full beard. He was intimidating to most people, but he'd always been sweet to me. I thought of him as a big teddy bear.

I hugged him tightly. He enjoyed holding me for a moment and then slowly pushed me away. "You gotta be careful, Nina. Raphe's hired me to spy on you. He told me if I saw you with any men I'm to rough 'em up."

I laughed at the ridiculous idea, but could see that he wasn't joking. I sighed loudly. "Oh no...I was starting to believe that this break-up went smoothly."

"Nah, you know that's not Raphe's way. He still sees you as his property."

"Yeah, me and every other girl who works at S&M." I groaned and sat down on the curb.

He plopped down beside me and put his arm around my shoulders. "If I wasn't afraid of Raphe, I'd ask you out myself, Nina. You know I think you're lovely and enjoy hearing you sing whenever I get the chance. I'm sad to see you go, but maybe it's best. That man is crazy, and crazy about you. It's a dangerous combination."

I leaned over and brushed my hand against his cheek in a playful way. He closed his eyes for a moment. And in that moment, I knew that he was in love with me...and I felt sad. I didn't feel the same way about him. "You are sweet. I still love that bastard, but he isn't good for me."

"I know, but I just got to let you know that I'm getting paid to follow you around so don't be offended. I'm just doing my job. I don't plan on reporting everything back to him...just so you know."

He winked at me, a playful smile on his face.

"I understand, Kal. Thanks for telling me." We stood and I hugged him goodbye. As I pulled away, there were a few moments of silence as he gazed at me lovingly. I leaned in and kissed him gently on the corner of the mouth. He was standing there in shock as I walked up the stairs and into my apartment. I filled out the application before I crashed for the night.

***

The next morning's interview was pleasant. Maurice was a very affable, large black man, almost jolly. He told me if I came back at 11pm, pimple-faced Tod would train me. He warned me that after a few days of training, I'd be on my own and that it could get scary. He warned me that the clientele at night was weirdos and druggies.

About 12 minutes into the first night, I'd already decided I hated Tod. He was a smart-ass who talked down to me. I'd encountered this type before. He explained the basics of cash register operation like I was a kindergartener.

I was so angry by my first smoke break, it was like I

had live bees in my underwear. "Just breathe," I told myself in a whispered tone. I suddenly felt a presence behind me and turned quickly, heart pounding through my chest.

A handsome, geeky fellow with glasses and spiky, black hair stood before me. He smiled. "Breathing is kind of important, isn't it?"

I was mesmerized, perplexed and intrigued by this handsome man. "Huh?" I managed to blurt out.

He laughed. "You were reminding yourself to breathe. It's kind of necessary to live, correct?"

I managed a nervous laugh. "Yes...it is." He gently touched a curly strand of my dark red hair softly and though I was a bit afraid that this stranger was being so bold, I couldn't move.

He leaned in close and whispered, "I would be sad if someone as beautiful as you stopped breathing."

I put out my cigarette and moved anxiously to the door. "My break's over. I have to go." I turned to walk towards the door and glanced back nervously, but he was gone.

***

The rest of the night went smoothly after I proved myself able to ring up customers without needing Tod. He sat behind me and read magazines while I did the rest of the work for the night. It worked out great for me since he ceased running his ugly, annoying mouth at me. It was mind-numbing work, but it paid better than working at McDonald's.

The only significant thing Tod said to me the rest of the night was after a group of scary-looking thugs came in and bought seven rolls of duct tape. They were dressed in ragged clothing and they had a wild look in their eyes. They didn't say a word, but I was visibly disturbed by their presence.

As soon as they left, Tod looked at me and snickered. "Aren't used to seeing the undead out and about, are you?"

I'd heard that there were vampires out there. All the freaks and geeks I'd ever hung out with believed in them. I wasn't sure I believed. The fact that there might be a whole pack, gang, or gaggle of them, (whatever the technical term is,) here in our town gave me pause.

He looked me straight in the eye. "You'd better get used to seeing them if you want to work here. We get at least a few deadies every night."

I started thinking back to all the years I'd worked at the nightclub and I'd never seen a vampire. Of course, I'd spent the majority of the time on the stage or backstage. I didn't get to mingle much. Raphe was jealous of the men who flocked to my curvy, pale body and blood-red hair.

Growing up, I'd never been a confident girl. Now, at 23, I knew the effect that I had on men and even a few women. It came in handy.

I shrugged it off. "Doesn't bother me." As long as they didn't follow me down a dark alleyway and suck my blood, I was cool with it.

2 THE SWING OF THINGS

The next few weeks flew by, and I didn't have to see Tod most of the time. Some nights he'd come in and do some stocking and paperwork, but most of the time I'd be on my own and I'd read or sing when there weren't any customers. Strangely, I never grew tired of singing, even when I was doing it for a living. Kal was still following me around, but he kept his distance. Some days I'd forget he was even there.

I had been an otherwise uneventful Thursday night when Raphe showed up unannounced. He waltzed up to the counter smugly as if he owned the place. "Enjoying your new career, little lady?"

It was a jab that really did hurt. He knew my dreams and my insecurities. Instead of replying, I glared at him. His satisfied smirk told me he knew he'd hit a nerve.

He continued his subtle attack. "Listen, let's get down to business. I'm willing to offer you the job back if you come home and try to work things out, Honey-Bunches. Some of the patrons even miss your sexy voice."

Anger was flaming up in my chest from the second he'd walked in and he kept adding more fuel. "I don't think that's a good idea. I know this job isn't glamorous, but I got it on my own merits and I don't have to deal with the owner ruling my personal life as well." I turned my back on him and started straightening some items behind the counter. I didn't want to let him know he was getting to me.

He raised an eyebrow and looked perturbed. "Well, enjoy your shit job, Nina. I got a line of lovely girls waiting to audition for your spot."

"Are you sure that all of them will be so willing to sleep with you as part of the audition process?" I spat the words like venom at him.

He grabbed my hair, roughly. For a moment, I was afraid. But then his face softened. He ran his fingers through my curls and smiled fiercely. "You'll wish you had accepted my extremely gracious offer." He walked out in a huff.

He might act like he could replace me that easily, but I had a loyal group of customers that came to see me at his club. I knew that he'd probably realized it was a mistake to fire me. I grinned like the Cheshire Cat just thinking about it, even though deep down, I was quite shaken by his visit.

A few minutes later, Kal actually came in. "Boss told me something I thought I'd relay to you."

"Okay?"

"This has got to be between the two of us because I could get fired...I trust you not to say anything, Nina. " He paused for my response.

"Sure."

"He said that some pretty lady came in earlier tonight and asked if she could buy out your contract.

Obviously, she don't know you're fired so he wanted to try and get you back because he could make a substantial amount of money off the deal."

"So that's why he wanted me back at work so bad...That asshole! I actually thought he missed me at least a little. I should have known better. He's always loved money more than me."

"I'm sure he does miss you, but yeah, he loves money."

"Do you happen to know who the lady was?"

"I don't know her name, but she said she wanted you for her club, Underland."

I pushed away from the counter and blinked at him. "Underland? But that's a goth club. Why would they want me to sing there? I don't know if I'd really fit in." Still, I was intrigued. "OK. Kal, thank you for telling me. I'll look into it."

"Of course, Nina. Be careful if you go to that place. It's a bit rough around the edges. There's punk sorts over there sometimes."

After he left, I thought about the idea of singing at Underland and it excited me. Even after I got home early that morning, I lay awake in bed and longed for having an audience to sing for again.

My curiosity was piqued. I had to go check it out. I decided to pay the club a visit on my next night off. Unfortunately, that was still several days away.

Who was this mysterious lady? Had she seen me sing before? Did she hear from some of my regulars? Why did she want me and what was this supposedly exorbitant price that made Raphe jump up and stand at attention? It was enough to grab my attention. My thoughts kept wandering back to all these questions over the next few days.

***

I spent my spare time in the store singing to keep my voice tuned up. I was going to go speak to someone about the job opportunity, but maybe they'd let me audition right there. Either way, I was ready to sing.

A few customers caught me in the act of singing. Some seemed impressed, but most seemed to find it a bit odd that I was singing lounge music in their corner convenience store.

Monday came and the day seemed to drag endlessly since I was off that night. I planned to go to the club so I picked out a little black dress that hugs my thighs and my spikiest heels. I cleaned the house frantically. I read half a book, but that couldn't hold my attention. I organized my shoes by color and style. I wiped down the bathroom mirror, but I could never get those streaks off. I tried to find things to do and ran out of them.

At last I felt it was late enough that I could get showered and dolled up. I was finished by 7, even though I knew things at the club wouldn't be hopping for another couple of hours at least.

I wondered if maybe I'd run into the mysterious lady if I got there earlier. I called a cab since it was on the other side of town. When I stepped outside to wait for the cab, Kal whistled at me. "Where you going, lady? You got a hot date?"

"Gonna check out Underland and see what's shakin'..." I waited for his reaction.

He just sighed. "I guess I'm going to have to follow

you. I ain't gonna report it but I need to know you are safe. I will stay outside, but just know I'm there if you need me, okay?"

I relaxed with a sigh. It was nice to know that he would be there. I was a bit nervous.

The cab pulled up to the curb. "Thank you, Kal. See you there." I leaned over and kissed him on the cheek before getting in.

About halfway there, I realized that I should have offered him a ride in my cab, but then again, it was Raphe paying for his transportation so maybe it was best to rip him off for a few more bucks. The idea thrilled me just a tiny bit.

When the cab came to a stop, I handed the driver his fare and peeked out the window. In front of me was a dark building made of large grey stone. It resembled a more modern version of a castle.

I thought maybe the place was closed because the street was deserted, but as soon as I touched the door handle, the door of the cab was opening and when I looked up, there was the handsome, geeky fellow from the first night at the store.

"Welcome to Underland, Nina."

"How did you…?" I was flabbergasted.

"Know your name? I've seen you perform more times than I can count. I am probably your most enthusiastic fan."

"Um, thank you…" I blushed for the first time in ages. I found it strange that I didn't remember ever seeing him at shows, but pushed the thought away. "Is it open?" I gestured at the deserted club door.

He chuckled lightheartedly. "Yes, it is open as long as it is dark outside. Come in."

I followed him in and as deserted as the street was, the inside was the quite the contrast. It was bustling with people…beautiful, dark, and interesting people.

When we walked in, several people near the entrance stopped talking and looked toward us. If there had been a jukebox, it would have stopped playing. My companion turned and grinned at me. Were they looking at me or him or the both of us? I was stunned and confused. After a few more awkward moments everyone turned their attention back to what they had been doing.

I turned my attention to the space around me. The room had a wealth of Greek columns and candelabras on every wall. All of the furniture was deep red. It was very Gothic-antique.

I was quickly falling in love with the place. This was further deepened the moment I saw the stage. A gorgeous upright piano sat on the left side of the stage, and in the center was an antique microphone. The curtain was white velvet accented with ornate black swirls. The stage itself was a dark rose-colored wood, possibly mahogany.

I gravitated straight to the front of the stage. I wanted to be on it. I fought the urge to climb the steps and sing. I turned and saw that I'd lost my fan. He was at the bar, but he was watching me from across the room. He seemed to take pleasure in my enjoyment of the place. Hopefully he'd missed the part where I was practically drooling with my mouth hanging open. I prayed this would be the job for me.

I straightened my shoulders and focused all my confidence. I sauntered up to him, trying my best to hold myself together. "Do you know the owner?"

"Of course I do."

"Can I meet her? I heard she might be interested in my singing abilities."

"That she is. She'll be out later and I'll introduce you. Right now, she's having a private dinner. Just have a seat and enjoy yourself in the mean time." He ushered me to a private booth on the right side of the stage area and got a waiter's attention. "Give this young lady any food or drink she desires, on the house."

I ordered a rum and coke. While waiting on the drink, I stared at this enchanting man. I tried to place him. He did seem familiar, but I couldn't place him at a show. I realized I didn't yet know his name. I strained to remember if he'd told me and I'd missed it, but I couldn't find mention in the recesses of my brain. "You...haven't told me your name."

"Ah, yes! Sorry, I've been distracted by your beauty. My name is Graham Olsen." He held out his hand and I shook it hesitantly. He continued enthusiastically. "Are you interested in coming to work here? It would certainly make the workplace more enjoyable for me."

"I guess it depends on if she wants me. So, what do you do here?"

"I don't strictly work "here", but I work as a messenger for Ilona."

"Ilona? Is that the owner?"

"Of course...you don't know of Ilona? I thought...you did." He looked slightly disappointed, but I wasn't sure why.

When the waiter came back with my drink, Graham excused himself and said he'd be back later. He slipped away in the blink of an eye and I suddenly felt very alone. The people at the next table gawked at me. I felt suddenly very aware of just how weird everyone was.

I had calmed considerably, but now I started to feel nervous again. I didn't really fit in here, yet the stage called to me. I wanted nothing more than to belong in this lush, dark environment. I wanted this to be my home.

A grey-haired old man got on stage and started

playing so softly and hauntingly that I melted into the music for a few moments. When the song ended, I was startled to find there was a beautiful woman standing in front of my booth who seemingly appeared out of nowhere.

"Hello. I am Ilona. I hear that you have come regarding my offer." There was a slight accent I could not place.

She sat down gracefully. I was in shock. I had never seen a woman so beautiful and delicate, yet so intimidating.

Her features made her seem stern and serious. She was thin, but had all the right curves. She was pale (like me), but she had shoulder-length, silky black hair. Her lips were painted red. They were not forming a smile or a frown. Her cheekbones seemed to be made of stone. I couldn't stop staring and I couldn't force words to come out of my mouth.

She smiled ever so slightly at me, knowingly. It was a bit unnerving. She leaned in slightly across the table. "Songstress, let us hear your lovely voice. At least speak to us," she jested with me.

"I...don't really know your offer, but I was told you tried to buy my contract. There is no contract." I licked my lips but found they were completely dry.

"Aha! I knew there was some reason he was being so antsy. I don't like that squirrelly little bastard." She leaned back in her seat with a satisfied smile. "Well, at least you are here now. I hope you will come work for us. I can't offer you much time, but you'll be reimbursed well. We have bands that play on Fridays and Saturdays. We would like to offer you $800 for performing each Sunday night - two shows per night. And we may also have some special events where we will also require your services. You will get more for those events."

I almost choked on my drink. One night a week for $800! I usually performed 4 nights a week at S&M, but was only paid $500 a week. I tried to play it cool. "When would you like for me to start? I will have to inform my current employer, of course."

"I would love it if you'd perform a single song for us now, songstress. Then report to us next Sunday at 11 p.m. for your first show at Midnight...and a second show at 3 a.m. A one hour set each time. You will ask any employee and they will show you to your private, guarded dressing room."

I was elated. I timidly approached the stage. The piano player stopped, as if he'd known I was coming. I leaned towards him and whispered, "Do you know 'Sway'?" He simply nodded and waited for me to approach the microphone.

I felt my heart in my throat, and wondered if the giant stage might swallow me whole. I adjusted the height of the mic stand as he started playing. No one was paying attention until I started singing. Instantly, a silent warmth filled the room. They were studying me, with a look of ecstasy on their faces. I thought it odd, but I was in the moment...feeling their love, their lust, and their enjoyment of my voice.

So, just like that, I had the job.

3 WHAT SHE WANTS, SHE GETS

When I stepped off the stage, I expected applause, but they were all in some kind of daze. They watched my every move. I got the impression that they enjoyed it, but it was odd not receiving immediate feedback. I walked toward the booth, but she was gone. A fresh drink was waiting along with a food menu. I was disappointed that Ilona wasn't there. I wanted to bask in her adoration and beauty a little longer.

The waiter came by a few minutes later. "Lady, you sing beautifully. The whole place is buzzing with talk about you. And it's all good."

"Thank you." I was dumbfounded by the attention.

It was a strange night.

"Ilona asked that you please order some food free of charge and that I give you this." He handed me a folded note. "I'm Reed, by the way. If you ever need anything while you are here, please ask me, Miss...?"

"Nina. Sure. I will." I flashed him my sexiest smile. I could tell he was flirting with me. He was cute. He had greased-back dirty blonde hair and he was the lanky build that I love. "Let me take a look at the menu."

He looked around anxiously at some of the other tables. "Sure. I'll be back in just a minute. Take your time." Just reading the menu made my mouth water. I ordered the herb-crusted oysters.

While I was waiting on my food, I unfolded the letter and a check fell out. It was for $1000. I gasped. The note was simple: "Your performance, though short, was well worth this. Go out and buy yourself some new clothes and we'll see you Sunday. Love, Ilona."

I came dangerously close to squealing out loud. I was getting paid before I even started. I didn't even know what to say or do. I glanced around so that I could thank her, but she was nowhere to be seen.

The oysters were orgasmic and I considered another drink, but eventually I rose to leave with great reluctance. I glanced around for any of the kind folks I had met, but didn't even see Reed. I used the bar phone to call a cab, which reminded me that I needed a new cell phone. I had trashed my old one after the break-up since he'd been paying for it anyway. Now I had a little bit of money and I was more than a little excited about getting a new one. My life had gone from sullen, lonely, and boring to exciting and busy in the course of one day. I had so much to do!

When I was about to get into my cab, Kal stepped out from the shadows. "Thank God you're okay, Nina. You were in there so long that I started to contemplate calling the boss."

"I'm fine. I got the job." I walked up to him and kissed him on the cheek. "Thank you." He pulled back from the kiss with a perplexed look on his face as I stepped into the cab.

***

As soon as I woke up the next morning, I walked down to the store and had a talk with Maurice. He seemed okay with the new job as long as I could still work there. He didn't want to lose me. I think he liked me because I had more brain cells than Tod. I was pretty sure Jell-O had more brain cells than Tod.

I spent the afternoon shopping. It may not have seemed like much money to some, but I felt like Julia Roberts in Pretty Woman. I picked out dresses in a wide array of styles and colors. I even bought my first iPhone. It all seemed so extravagant. I was excited I could catch up on a few bills, but my insecurities kept creeping up on me. I felt like I should hoard some of the money away in case this didn't work out. I desperately wanted to succeed at this job.

The next few days I was stuck at the store or at home. It was pure torture. I could almost hear the clocks ticking everywhere I went; the time was going in slow-motion. I wanted Sunday night to arrive fast. I had my outfit planned and my makeup bags packed to take with me to my very own dressing room.

I called Grandma Mae Sunday afternoon. I'd been raised by Grandma Mae. She is my father's mother and raised me because my parents hadn't really the time or interest for child-rearing. I was an only child, quiet and introspective. I think Grandma Mae enjoyed my company. I tried to be as helpful as I could because she was the only family I truly felt anything for and I was always scared she would abandon me too. I spent some summers and other random times with my parents in Alabama, but I grew to hate it there. Even though I'd visit for a short time, I was always treated like a burden.

She answered the phone, "Hello Sunshine." She's the only person I let get away with calling me that.

"Hi Gramma, how did you know it was me?"

"Either I've turned psychic in my old age. Or I got me a caller i.d. One of those."

I giggled. She was such a smartass, but in an endearing way. "Well, I know I have been bad and haven't called you since Raphe and I broke up but I have some news…"

"Good, I hope?" she queried cheerfully.

"Yes! Very good! I got a job at a different club...making much better money!"

"It's not a strip club, is it, Honey? I mean, I don't have no problem with the girls at those establishments, but I'd rather you not do it."

I loved her, but she could be blunt and abrasive at times. "No, Gramma. It's an upscale club. Even nicer than Smoke & Mirrors. You'll be happy to know that I'm singing, not stripping."

"Great, darlin'. I'm so proud."

From there, she informed me of every minute detail of everything going on in her rural southern life: what the neighbors were doing, who the neighbors were doing, etc. By the end of the conversation I was exhausted.

Since there were hours left until my shift, I set my alarm and took a nap. I dreamed of Ilona. She was touching my hand gently and helping me onto the stage. There were cheers and whistles coming from a crowd I could not see. When I started to sing, the microphone fell over. A group of thugs pulled me off the stage. I glanced back at Ilona but she wasn't there. Despite the negative overtones of the dream, I woke with a smile. I was only thinking of Ilona's touch.

When I arrived at the club, Kal was waiting outside for me. He wished me luck as I dashed in the door. Everyone stared at me again when I walked in, but it didn't get quiet this time. There were hushed whispers all around the room. I was wowed yet again with the look and feel of the place. The lush atmosphere could make you forget this was considered a punk/goth club. My nerves were on fire. Everyone looked busy. I didn't know who to ask about the dressing room. I looked around at various doors and tried to figure it out myself.

A waiter walked past me hurriedly, but I managed to catch him. "Sir, where are the dressing rooms?"

He seemed perturbed but answered me politely. "See that hallway over there where the restrooms are?"

"Uh-huh..."

"At the end of the hallway is a guarded door. The dressing rooms are in the hallway beyond that if you are authorized to enter."

Well, that sounded ominous. "Thanks."

I hurried that way, worried that I wouldn't have time to touch up my makeup. The guard looked familiar to me, but I couldn't place his face. He apparently knew me. "Come right in, Miss Vernon. We've been expecting you. The last door on the left is your dressing room, directly across the hall is Ilona's office. Do not disturb her in her office unless you have been invited by her to go in." - another ominous statement to ponder.

It grew colder the deeper I got into the long hallway. They apparently kept the rest of the club at arctic temperatures. I passed a few doors along the way but they were all closed. I heard no noise to indicate the rooms were occupied. Fluorescent lights flickered overhead. The hallway was unadorned. It was just grey stone walls and dull gold carpet.

I gasped when I opened the door and found an antique vanity with a matching armoire in a large room with an exquisite red velvet couch and matching chair. It was the classic vanity with the soft white bulbs all around the mirror, just like I'd dreamed of as a child. S&M just had a cloudy old mirror and a few rusty folding chairs in a room the size of a broom closet.

I never wanted anything more than to sing. I'd been singing from the moment I could talk. Grandma Mae loved to tell stories about how I'd entertained guests with song and dance routines starting at age 3. So, as you can see, this was very important to me. It was in my very soul to sing.

I laid down my things and just relaxed on the couch for a few seconds. I couldn't believe this. It was like a dream. It sounds silly, but I felt like I was one step away from Carnegie Hall! As soon as I was comfortable, there was a knock at the door.

"Come in?"

Reed peeked in with the door just cracked a few inches. "Ms. Vernon, do you need anything before show-time? You're on in 40 minutes. I was told to ask if you need food, drink, or anything else…"

"Nina, please. Call me Nina."

"Sure." He winked at me. "Whatever you wish."

"Do you have tea? I really need a hot drink for my voice. If not, coffee or something else...lemon & honey if you have that."

"I'm sure we can find some tea." He smiled reassuringly at me. "You'll be fine, by the way. And if you haven't noticed, there is a door leading to the back of the stage over there." He motioned to a dark corner of the room where there was a curtain. "That's where you will enter at show-time. Someone will come get you when it's time."

"Thanks." I turned to smile at him as he left.

He ran off and I did the finishing touches on my hair and makeup. It almost felt like I was a child playing dress up and found myself wondering who the silly girl in the mirror was. Could I really pull this off? My heart started pounding so hard I could feel it in my teeth. When Reed brought the tea, I thought I wouldn't be able to drink it because I was shaking like a wet dog.

I got up and walked over to the curtain. Behind it was an actual door. I opened it and found yet another hallway. I followed the hallway of even more doors and it came out to the left side backstage. I hurried back to the dressing room. I wasn't sure I was supposed to be back there and the silence was a little creepy.

I sat back down on the couch and just tried to do breathing exercises. When it was only about 5 more minutes to show-time, I stood up to glance at myself in the mirror and started pacing the room. A knock at the door startled me. It was a guard come to escort me to the stage. He walked me all the way to the entrance at the back left of the stage and stood there. I thought I might pass out. But I heard a voice introduce me and suddenly, nothing mattered. Like a switch, I turned on that magic something that made me a performer. I was ready. I took a deep breath and stepped out on the stage.

At the end of the first song, I took a moment to scan and gauge the audience. In the back of the room was Kal, sitting nervously at the bar away from everyone else. The place was packed. At the very front of the stage sat Ilona, Graham, and a group of large, intimidating men. One other girl sat at the table: a timid-looking blonde girl. She was pretty, but she looked out of place.

I did a one hour set. The crowd was silent and

dazed again. I wasn't sure how to take it. After the last song, Ilona started clapping, then Graham and everyone else joined in. My heart soared to find that Ilona had enjoyed my music. I breathed a sigh of relief and curtsied, then slipped backstage and into the dressing room.

I had a change of clothes, but I suddenly felt like what I'd brought wasn't fancy enough. I stayed in my lovely red and black flamenco-style dress. I sat on the couch and just enjoyed the cool, tomb-like air of the dressing room. After the oppressing heat of the stage lights, it was marvelous.

There was a knock. I found myself hoping it was Ilona. I freshened my lipstick in a hurry. "Come in."

Ilona floated into the room gracefully. Her entourage looked offended when she shut the door right behind her, leaving them in the hallway. Graham looked terribly disappointed. She expressed how wonderful and mesmerizing and lovely I was. I basked in her attention. I thanked her for having me. She touched a soft red curl that was out of place on my head. I shivered.

She leaned in close and stated in a matter of fact

tone, "You will join us for drinks. Food too, if you wish." And then she waltzed out.

Graham peeked in the door the second she was gone. He was looking particularly dapper. He had always been wearing a suit when I'd seen him, but that night he was wearing a neatly-pressed, brown pin-striped suit. "Wonderful, as always."

"Thank you, kind sir." I fake-curtsied for him and he seemed to follow my every movement with his eyes. His eyes were a lovely light-brown. I usually didn't notice a man's eyes unless they were a startling blue or green, but his eyes were kind.

"Are you joining us?"

"Do I have a choice?" I asked meekly.

He didn't respond but kind of shrugged.

"Mhmm, I'll be out in just a few moments." I glanced around to look for something that needed to be done.

He pressed his lips together tightly. "Sit by me?"

"We shall see." I shot him a whimsical grin.

I let my hair down and had a quick lie down on the couch before joining them. They were discussing my voice when I walked up. The word "mesmerizing" came up again.

I approached cautiously and stammered out a hello.

Ilona told the blonde, sternly, to move to an empty seat across the large, round table. The blonde glanced at me with a flash of anger as she obliged, but she kept quiet. And so I was seated next to Ilona. Graham was on the other side of her and he looked a bit hurt. Hopefully he would understand since she was my boss and I cared more about keeping her pleased.

And then there was the fact that Ilona dominated my thoughts. I wanted to touch her perfect, silky black hair. I'd thought many women were attractive, but I'd never been quite this bewitched with a female before. I was confused, but excited. Her eyes were almost a steel blue-green. I hadn't noticed before, but they were quite seductive. When she laughed, they were so light they made me think of winter skies.

There were multiple conversations going on.

Though there were at least a dozen other people at the table, I was lost in Ilona. Occasionally, she'd glance my way when she wasn't speaking to the others. Without warning, she shouted for a waiter and I almost jumped out of my skin. Her voice raised was like an angry banshee. I was suddenly pondering how frightening she would be if she was actually angry.

A waiter came running over. "Yes, Mistress?"

She waved her hand at me in an elegant manner. "Get this young lady anything she desires - and make it quick."

He looked at me and I smiled. "I'll have the herb-crusted oysters and some water, please."

Ilona looked a bit annoyed at me. "Water? Everything you eat or drink here is free of charge. Order whatever you like. I had fancied getting you drunk tonight." She laughed. I was equal parts scared and excited by this flirty little joke. Did this job just get better or what?

I blushed. "Oh...um...I'll have your best red wine, please. But also bring the water. I need it for my voice."

I ate and chit-chatted with the others at the table. Graham just stared at me while I spoke and frankly, the rest of the time as well. I was pretty sure I had more than one admirer at the table. It was slightly intimidating.

My 3 am show came quickly. I went back to the dressing room again for a few minutes. I checked myself in the mirror and decided to put my hair back up. The curls had a bad habit of being unruly. I came up to the stage a few minutes early again. I peeked out of the curtain. Most of the crowd was miraculously still there at 3 am. Was it for me or was it just the hours these people kept?

I stepped on the stage promptly and gave the piano man a list of songs. I was never given a name for him and he never spoke. He just nodded at the songs he knew. I mixed up the songs to keep it fresh. I got the same reaction as earlier - complete attention from the room, but a chilling silence. It seemed like no one moved or breathed during my performance. At the end, applause gradually built up until the whole room joined. This would take some getting used to.

When I packed up my things and came out of my dressing room, Ilona and her entourage were gone. I was a bit disheartened not to see her again, but I was also exhausted.

As soon as I stepped outside, Kal caught me by the shoulder. He looked shaken to the core and he spoke hurriedly in hushed tones. "You can't come back here. You're in danger!"

"Is it Raphe? Did he find out or something?"

He looked ready to tuck me under his arm and run when he said, "It is so much worse than that. I noticed some odd things while I was inside so I made a few calls. This club is run by vampires - including that chick who hired you. The whole place is crawling with undead!"

"What? That's insane...Why would you say that? Everyone here has been so nice to me. Did Raphe put you up to this?"

"No, but if you keep coming here I'm going to have to tell him. I fear for your safety, Nina."

All of a sudden there was a whoosh of air beside me and the next thing I knew Graham was holding Kal up in the air like he was nothing. "You will tell no one what you know of this place and you will NOT inform her former boyfriend about where she is working or what she is doing. Do you understand me?"

Kal squeaked out "Yessir."

Graham put him down and moved closer to me. "Are you okay?" Kal rushed away, but still threw some furtive glances back at Graham.

I was in a state of shock. "I don't...was he telling the truth?" I was confused by what I had just witnessed. Graham was a very thin man and Kal was...bulky.

"Yes. Some of the people in the club are vampires...including myself and Ilona. I hope this doesn't frighten you away. We do not wish you harm. In fact, quite the opposite on my part." His smile was clearly meant to reassure me, but the shock was so great that I couldn't even speak.

After a moment he spoke again. "Your voice takes us for a ride through places and emotion that we have not visited since we were human. You have a gift beyond normal singing ability."

I sighed. If this was true, it explained a lot about the

reaction I got from the audience in the club. "Thank you. I don't know how I feel about all this, but I'm exhausted and forgot to call a cab. Can you call one for me?"

"Of course." He got his cell phone out of his pocket and walked a few feet away to make the call.

I sat down on the curb and stared off into space for a moment. I knew there was the possibility that vampires existed, but finding out they were surrounding me in my new workplace was a bit overwhelming. It was too much to handle and I just wanted to go home, rest, and think on it.

A nice BMW pulled up to the curb beside us and a guy got out and handed Graham the keys. He looked at me. "No need for a cab. I can take you." I looked at him hesitantly and tossed me a flirty smile. "I promise I won't bite." This was a terrible joke to make at that moment, but despite this, I still snickered.

On the way to my apartment, he tried to make small talk, but I was feeling tired and intimidated. I wasn't much for conversation. We were close to my street when I realized I had not told him where I lived, but he seemed to be heading that direction. "How do you know where I live?"

He sighed. "I checked you out for Ilona before she made the job offer. I'm sorry if this offends or frightens you, but she would not have hired you if she didn't know a few things about you first. "

"Oh."

He pulled up in front of my building and I got out. He ran around the car and tried to open the apartment door for me. "Can I come up and help you with anything? Would you like to talk more?"

"No thanks." He looked crestfallen, and turned to leave. Seeing how much Graham cared for me...it made me realize that vampires have feelings too.

His sadness was a reality check. I decided to keep the job at least for a while longer. If anything weird or scary happened, I would leave. But deep down, I didn't want to leave. I loved the place and despite what I now knew; I wanted more time with the mysterious Ilona.

I slept my way through the next day, then moped around the house for a few days because I was off from the store. I didn't know what to do with myself. I found myself longing for the attention of the club crowd.

I was still a bit creeped out by the vampire thing, and by Graham's apparent stalking of me. I wondered how much was actually Ilona and how much was his obvious interest in me. I also pondered what he had said of my voice. Would this not be the case with any good singer? I wasn't sure. I would make it a point to ask more about that at a later date.

***

When I went back to work at the store things were uneventful, aside from Tod asking me questions about the club because Maurice had told him about my new job. He mentioned possibly coming to see me sing some time. I told him I didn't think it was a good idea. It almost felt like he was trying to hit on me, but if that's what he was trying to accomplish, he was doing a poor job of it.

Once he left for the night, I kept noticing more people that came in were staring at me lustfully and I started to get nervous. What was going on? Normally, I loved attention, but I felt I had attracted the wrong kind and became fearful. I couldn't help but feel like a piece of meat tossed into a wolves' den. I also found myself trying to figure out which customers were vampires, but I couldn't be sure.

I hadn't seen Kal since that night outside Underland. I hoped he was safe. Surely he wasn't stupid enough to try anything with the vampires, but I worried about what he may have told Raphe. Then again, if he didn't tell him anything of my goings-on, would Raphe start to question his loyalty? If so, then he'd most certainly not be safe. I hoped to see or hear from him soon just to know he was okay. He was a good guy. He was just trying to protect me.

Friday night, I decided to drop in at the club before work just because I missed it. Plus, I felt the need to let Graham know that I was okay with everything. The club was crowded and there was an awful, loud punk band on stage. Well, the crowd seemed into it, but it wasn't my kind of music. It's stupid, but I kept thinking that they didn't belong on my stage. It didn't make sense, but I couldn't help but feel that I owned that stage.

I looked around and didn't spot any of the people I knew. Not even Reed was in sight. I asked the bartender if Graham or Ilona were around. He told me Ilona was out for the night. He wasn't sure about Graham, but said he'd call him.

I sat down in a booth. I suddenly regretted coming unannounced. I felt a wave of loneliness hit me. Just as my eyes were starting to water, a waiter came up. "Miss Vernon, the bartender told me to tell you that Graham was taking care of some business, but would be here as soon as possible. Also, is there anything I can get you?"

"A Tom Collins and a food menu, please." I smiled at him.

He ran off to fetch those for me and I waited for Graham. As much as I liked Ilona, I couldn't discount Graham. He was a handsome guy. He was geeky, but it worked. He seemed very confident and intelligent, two attractive qualities in a man.

I had certainly thought about him, but he was worlds away from Ilona. I knew that I couldn't be the only one to have worshipped at Goddess Ilona's feet. She was powerful and beautiful, which made her extremely alluring. I'd never met a woman who charmed me this much. An image of her biting my neck flashed in my mind. I started to feel aroused, but also embarrassed. I was hoping right then that no one could pick up my brain waves.

This is, of course, when Graham showed up.

4 VAMPIRE 101

Graham was out of breath, but he looked positively giddy to see me. He sat across from me and just stared at me for a moment or two before he spoke. "I didn't expect you tonight, or frankly ever again, but I'm thrilled you are here."

"I wasn't sure if I wanted to come back at first. This place has its charms. I am still a bit uneasy about the whole thing, but I am not quite ready to give up my new job."

He gave the waiter an annoyed sidelong glance when he interrupted our conversation. I tried to stifle a giggle. This guy had it bad. I was flattered that such a striking gentleman cared for me, but even more impressed that he was a vampire interested in a mere mortal. Or was he even interested for romantic reasons? I wasn't sure quite how this worked. Maybe he wanted me for dinner. Either way, I enjoyed his attention.

I ordered a steak this time. I wanted to try something different and I was extremely hungry. I wasn't sleeping or eating well because I was consumed with thoughts about the club and my new acquaintances.

When the waiter was gone again, I confronted Graham with my thoughts. "How many times have you been to my apartment or followed me?"

He looked worried. "Um...You want a number? More times than I could count." It was just as I suspected and I now had chill bumps. Thanks, Mr. Creepy-pants.

I sighed deeply, braced myself, and looked him in the eye. "Tell me more about vampires."

"What do you want to know?" He looked wary of my line of questioning.

I couldn't tell if I was treading in dangerous waters and nearing some secret thing that shouldn't be mentioned, but I continued anyway. "How long have vampires existed? How much of the movie stuff is real? Stuff like that..."

"Just the basics, then, eh?"

I nodded.

"Well, that's simple. Ilona's the oldest vampire that I have met. She is not the first. Vlad Tepes was the oldest known vampire, but even he had a creator. Not much history is known before him. It was even more of a secret subject then than it is now. Um...sunlight is painful because it deteriorates the fragile skin, but it can't kill just from a small amount of exposure."

His eyes darted quickly around the room before he continued. "Garlic does nothing. It's just stinky. Stakes through the heart and many other injuries that would kill a human can be deadly depending on the age of the vampire. The newer the vampire; the easier it is to kill them. The only true way to be certain if you have killed a vampire is to sever the head from the body."

"What about mirrors?"

He laughed. "We show up in mirrors. I think the reason for that myth is the fact that people have so many fears and superstitions about mirrors already. I have given it a little thought. Vampires tend to sneak up on victims quite easily. I'm sure you can imagine seeing nothing in the mirror and then turning around to find a monster. For those who survived, they must have wondered why they never saw the predator in the mirror. Turns out, the predator is very sneaky and very fast. That's all."

"How old are you?"

"Do you mean my true birth or when I became a vampire?"

"Both?"

"I was born in 1891 and became a vampire in 1922."

"Wow." My jaw dropped. I pondered on this for a minute, rendered speechless. "Ok, how do you feed? Do you actually kill people for blood?"

"Most do not kill...at least not anymore. It brings too much attention to us. It's against our rules. Some don't follow the rules and are hunted by our kind. We usually find willing donors in lovers. We don't need a lot of blood. Just a small taste to keep the appetites at bay."

"Where are your fangs? I have not noticed a single set of fangs since I've been here."

He threw back his head and laughed really hard. "Not everyone in the club is a vampire. Our fangs are further back than the canine teeth. Yet again, not like what you see in the movies. I have a theory that it's evolution's way of protecting us from being discovered." He pulled his lips taut at his cheek and I saw the sharp fangs, but for some reason I found them sexy. I blushed a little. I didn't expect that reaction. You would think I'd be horrified and not aroused. I wondered how his fangs would feel on my neck.

"Interesting." I glanced down, embarrassed by where my questions had led me.

He looked at me smugly as though he knew what I was thinking. I hoped he wasn't aware of my thoughts. My food came and I inhaled it. It seemed like every time I ate the food at Underland that I was eating my first meal in weeks. I made a mental note to meet and thank the cook someday.

He just watched me peacefully and patiently while I ate. He didn't speak while I was eating. I wonder if he thought it was disgusting or if he missed the enjoyment of partaking in food.

I noticed something while I was enjoying my steak. The little blonde girl who was seated by Ilona at the table during my performance was playing bass in the punk band. I was impressed. She'd seemed so timid. I was curious about her. "Graham, who is the blonde?"

He groaned. "That is Ilona's girlfriend, Topaz. She is the spoiled brat of the place. Her band is called "Fangs For All The Fish".

"Oh." I tried not to look disappointed. "Is she human?"

"Yes. Most relationships are vampire and human. Vampires have relationships with other vampires sometimes but it never lasts long. We get bored and our tempers tend to flare up with each other. It's the less than charming side of being around vampires." He looked past me as though he was lost in thought. "Human lovers will put up with it either out of fear or because of the novelty of being with a vampire. Other vampires will just walk away."

"How long have they been in a relationship?"

He calculated in his head for a split-second. "Almost a year, I think. I haven't been keeping track. She lives here at the club with Ilona. She was a teen runaway. We're not sure how old she is. She said she was 17 when she first came." He paused with his brow furrowed. "We're not even sure if Topaz is her real name. We've tried to do some research on her, but so far we've found nothing."

"She lives here?" For some reason, I pictured her sleeping on the couch in my dressing room and I didn't like it.

"Sure. So do I. Ilona and her entire entourage have little apartments below the club."

"Gotcha...creepy basement tombs."

He chuckled and I looked at him with a raised eyebrow. He stopped laughing because of the look I was giving him. "There are no windows on the basement level. There's no need for coffins. The apartments are very basic since we don't have your human needs, but they are very much apartments and we all decorate them in our own style just like you would."

"I would like to see one some time."

He grinned. "You can see mine tonight if you wish."

My face started to turn a bright shade of pink so I glanced at my watch nervously. "Uh...no. Not tonight. I've got to go to work. Maybe another time." I cleared my throat. "Can you please tell Ilona I stopped by and was sad to miss seeing her?" And there was that crestfallen look again. I stood up and walked away without a backwards glance. I couldn't stand to see the hurt I knew I would find on his face.

***

The rest of the weekend dragged leading up to Sunday. I wondered if it would always be this way. Would I always be waiting every moment in painful slow-motion when I wasn't at Underland? I wondered if my obsession with the place and the people of Underland was becoming unhealthy. I couldn't make it stop. I also felt like I needed to keep the secret of the club. I had no friends anymore so that part would be easy.

All of my friends worked at Smoke & Mirrors. It was my world because of my relationship with Raphe. Now they were off-limits because they were his employees and his friends. It just wasn't possible to be close to any of them at that moment.

Sunday afternoon I contemplated calling Grandma Mae again, but was afraid spilling my guts to her about everything going on would just make her worry. I decided against that and I napped instead.

It seemed like I was sleeping a lot more than normal on my days off from the club. Either the stress of working at a vampire club was getting to me or I was depressed. Possibly a combination of the two? I was only depressed when I was away from Underland.

When I arrived that night, I went straight back to the dressing room. There were red roses with no note. There was a fancy covered silver platter with my hot tea and herb-crusted oysters. I had that warm and fuzzy feeling inside. Someone was going out of their way to make me feel welcome. I wondered who it was.

The performance went smoothly again. I joined Ilona and her entourage at the table afterwards for a round of praise. I noticed that the blonde wasn't there. Just using it for chit-chat, I asked, "Where is Topaz this evening?"

Silence fell as all eyes turned to Ilona.

"She's gone. She won't be back," she said coldly. I tried to look for a hint of care in her eyes, but there wasn't any.

No one dared to talk for what seemed like an eternity. Finally, Graham cleared his throat and spoke. "Nina, how are you liking it here?"

"Oh, I love the place, the people, and the food is great too!" I gushed. I truly meant that, but I was more enthusiastic that I intended because Ilona was near and I was felt pressure to please her.

Ilona smiled. "I have some business to attend to, but I assure you I will try my best to check out the second show." She rose and walked away. The entourage followed shortly. Graham was the only one left. I turned to him. "Do you think I offended her by what I said?"

He thought for a moment on this before replying. "I don't think so. She just has a lot on her mind. She's heard rumor that some of her own have been killing locally. She's not happy and she doesn't know who it is either. It will take some investigation. There are other things as well that I have been asked not to speak of."

"Does it have something to do with the blonde?"

"You could say that." He looked extremely unhappy.

I rose from the table. "I'm going to get ready for the next show." I'd had too much awkwardness for one night.

I had a lie down on the couch. Were all vampires so full of drama?

***

I had shut my eyes for what seemed like a few moments when there was a gentle rapping at the door. Ilona entered without waiting for a response. She practically floated from the door to the couch and sat right beside my feet. She started rubbing my feet gently. Despite the fact that her fingers were like ice, her touch was exquisitely tender. Her silence was a bit unnerving. After a few minutes, she finally spoke. "I'm so glad to hear that you are enjoying your stay here. I don't want this to feel like work, but more like a home. If there is anything I can do for you, please tell me."

"I...I...am loving it here. So far everything is wonderful." I stuttered because I was nervous just being this close to her and she was touching me on top of that. It was sensory overload!

"I hope that we can become...closer." She practically whispered the last word and my heart leaped a little in my chest, partially from excitement and partially from fear, but I couldn't help but wonder what she meant. She was still my boss and I didn't want to ask.

I couldn't think straight right that second. My brain was searching for an appropriate response and coming up empty.

Without warning, Graham came in the slightly ajar door and my heart sunk. I felt a sudden flash of guilt like he was catching us in the act of something much worse because I knew he wouldn't react well.

He didn't say or do anything. He just turned around and walked back out.

I opened my mouth to say something, but stopped. I'm not sure why it plagued me to know that I had hurt him. He and I were just friends, but his attention did flatter me.

Ilona gave a quick goodbye and floated elegantly out of the room.

**

The next night at the store, I was fighting sleep. It was completely dead in there, no pun intended. My eyes closed for what could have been minutes but felt like a split second. When I opened my eyes, Graham was standing in front of the counter. I was so startled that I almost fell off the stool I was seated on.

"Dear God, you scared the shit out of me!"

"Sorry, but I had to see you. We need to talk. Look...I see the way you look at Ilona. If you get involved with her, there is something you must know." He studied my face. "Rumor has it that she kills her lovers when she's done with them. I don't know if that's what happened to Topaz, but I do know that every lover she's had since I've been around her has mysteriously disappeared."

I felt the anger rise in me as he spoke. "I don't buy that. Ilona has been very kind to me. This is just a rumor that you speak of. You come at me with no evidence of these things. Don't you know better than to spread rumors?" I wanted to scream at him to leave me alone. I was a little scared that this might be true, but I wasn't hearing it because of my developing feelings for her. "Besides, wouldn't she get caught if she had? Against the rules and all that, ya know?"

"Ilona is more powerful and influential than you know. No one wants to risk investigating her and getting themselves on her bad side. I just want you to be careful. I realize you are an adult and can make your own decisions. I just want to protect you from harm...always."

"You can't always be there when I'm in trouble." I really wanted to bring up that perhaps his point of view was skewed by his attraction to me, but I was not that mean.

"But I have...nevermind." He sullenly trudged out

of the store.

I was angry that he was trying to keep me from Ilona, but at the same time I liked him as well and did not want him to hurt for me. I needed some time to cool down.

Luckily, I had the rest of the night in an empty store. I still hadn't seen Kal around. I decided to make a few phone calls about that soon. I had to know if he was okay.

5 TIME TO THINK

Over the next few days, I'd thought about all the things Graham had said. Maybe I didn't know Ilona and if she was capable of such a horrible thing, but I was still willing to give her the benefit of the doubt. Even so, the reaction I got when asking about Topaz was very strange indeed. I even considered asking her about it privately, but she was a vampire and I'd like to think I wasn't that stupid.

For once I didn't find myself wishing for Sunday. I was confused by everything going on. I still wanted to perform. The desire for that never left me, but I started to wonder if this vampire scene was really for me. It seemed like a lot of stress. I was a mess that whole week. I was up and I was down and everywhere in between. Just when I thought I was going to be okay, my mind would find a way to spin the situation and I would sink into a depression. Could Ilona be a cold-blooded killer? Could Graham be feeding me this line of thought for his own purposes? I was stumped.

On Wednesday, I called Patricia. She was a blonde waitress at Smoke & Mirrors. She was one of the few who, I think, had not slept with Raphe. We'd talked a few times, but I wouldn't say we were friends.

"Hi, Patricia. This is Nina. How are things?"

"Nina! Things are okay. How are you? I heard you were working at a convenience store. Please tell me that is not true. I hate to think of you wasting your talent working at a crummy old corner shop."

I mulled it over and quickly decided that telling her about Underland wasn't a good idea. "I'm afraid it's true, doll. Don't worry, things are looking up. Listen, have you seen Kal lately? He was coming by the store regularly, but he hasn't been by this week. I was just hoping he was okay." I bit my lip while I waited for her to respond.

"Kal's fine. Raphe's got him working a lot since Dean got fired."

I let out a big sigh of relief. Thank God! I thought I'd gotten a friend killed. "How's Raphe doing?"

"He got over your pretty quick. He's on to Akila."

"Wow. Akila, really? She's like 12."

"She's 19, Nina, but I know what you mean. I heard that he's frustrated over finding an act to replace you though. He can't seem to find anyone as good if that makes you feel any better.

"Yes, yes it does." I smiled smugly and wrapped up the conversation. "Thanks for chatting with me, Patricia. Tell Kal I said 'Hi'."

The next Sunday night, the only person present who was familiar at all was Reed. Ilona and her entire entourage missed my performances. I was sad, but as the saying goes, "the show must go on."

The crowd was receptive, in their own weird way, as usual. I didn't even bother to ask anyone where the vampires were. I assumed it was important business and tried not to dwell on my concerns that maybe they had already grown tired of me.

My depression worsened that week. I didn't have my true "Underland fix". I called in at the store on Monday. I felt fatigued, but I was sure it's just from not getting out of bed most of the day. Underland was throwing extreme negatives and positives at me. I wasn't sure how I felt about it.

Should I just run away from the vampire's den? That was the question that plagued me for that week away from my beloved vampires. They were something new and exotic in my life and I was back to feeling like a Plain Jane.

Even though our last few visits were strained, I even found myself wishing Graham would stop by the store or my apartment to check on me. Any contact from the wonderful world of vamps would have at least given me peace. But he never came. Had I wounded him too deeply on our last encounter? I knew he cared for me, but I wasn't sure I understood how deeply.

Again I felt lonely. There wasn't a single person I trusted to tell these secrets to or get advice from. I needed to make friends outside the club. I realized I shouldn't make the same mistake I did at Smoke & Mirrors. Where does one make friends? This thought weighed on my mind for a few days.

Thursday I woke up around 10 a.m. and scraped myself out of bed; I was determined to do something for my sanity. I wandered into a coffee shop a few buildings down from my apartment. I'd been by it a million times, but never gone in. I sipped on a mocha and watched the people come and go. It was very therapeutic. I was seeing normal people living their normal lives. I was there for hours.

People came and went, but one person was also there the whole time. She was an overweight brown-haired girl who looked at least somewhat close to my age. She was sitting at her laptop typing non-stop since before I'd arrived. She would only briefly stop to stare at the screen, deep in thought. I tried to talk myself into going over to speak to her, but I was scared and worried about interrupting her. Out of everyone I'd seen, she was the only one I was remotely interested in. I related to creative types and she was obviously a writer.

I bit the bullet. I thought to myself "Please, be my friend," as I leaped up from my seat and walked over and sat down at her table. "Hope I'm not bothering you, but I'm curious. What are you writing?"

She looked up nervously. "A romance novel."

"Oh. You looked frustrated. Want to talk about it?"

She shoved her laptop away. "Sure. Maybe it will help. I'm only a few chapters in, but it's appallingly obvious that I haven't had any real romance in my life in a long time. I need inspiration." She grinned at me.

"I'm Olivia, but everyone calls me Liv. What's yours?"

"Nina. Olivia is a lovely name. How long have you been writing? Is this your first novel?" I was excited. I hoped I wouldn't scare her off with so many questions.

"I've been writing poetry my whole life and have always intended to write a novel, but just never found the time. My love life has been dead for a few months so I figure there is never a time like the present. Plus I keep edging closer to 30 and I worry that if I don't do it now, I'll never do anything with my life."

"You're almost 30? You don't look it."

"I'll be 29 in December. Thank you. I feel old as dirt. How old are you?"

"23." I suddenly felt intimidated by our age difference, but I wanted so desperately for her to be my friend.

She glanced at her watch. "Oh shit! I've got a meeting to attend. I'll catch up with you another time. I'm usually here mid-mornings on Tuesdays and Thursdays." She shouted, "It was nice to meet you!" as she ran out the door. I thought it went well. I knew where to see her and that gave me hope.

***

I was feeling absolutely giddy when I left the coffee shop. When I got home, I cleaned my apartment. My depression had left my apartment and life a disaster area. I knew that it wasn't magically going to go away, but at least I had something to look forward to. I had a light at the end of the tunnel. Could I confide in her? God, I hoped I could. I desperately needed someone to talk to.

Kal came by that night at the store while I was

stocking. "Hey, Nina. I heard you asked about me."

I glanced up at him from where I was sitting on the floor, stocking canned goods. "Oh, I'm so glad to see you're okay, Kal. I was worried after that night...I'm so sorry about what happened." I stood up so we could talk. I wrapped my arms around his large body. I was relieved that he was alive and well.

"You don't have to apologize. I know hearing that was a shock to you. I'm glad you are safe. Does this mean you've quit that place?"

"Um...no. For the moment, I'm sticking with it. Maybe I can if I find something else down the road. Don't worry, I'm safe." I glanced down. I felt like I was telling a lie to myself as well as him.

"I'll be back to tailing you as soon as they hire a new bouncer. I'm working every night since Dean got fired."

"So, Raphe hasn't given up, yet? That's ridiculous." I chuckled. "What happened to Dean? Patricia told me he'd been fired but not why…"

He looked grim. "He said things have gone to shit

since you've been gone. Everyone else was thinking it, but Dean is the only one who had the balls to say it. We got less customers. Raphe is irritated to the point where he snaps at everyone. We are all on edge...just waiting for the ship to go down."

"Oh." I looked away. Dean was a nice guy. I hated hearing that I might have inadvertently caused him to lose his job.

"I'll be seeing you again real soon, Nina." I gave him a quick goodbye hug and watched him walk out the door.

The great day I'd been having melted away with a wave of guilt, but there was nothing to be done.

***

That Sunday, I was greeted at the curb by Graham, who opened the door of the cab for me when I arrived. I thought he'd hated me after our last encounter. "Hello, Miss Lovely." He grabbed my hand to help me out, and then he gently kissed it. I shivered. I wanted desperately to ask if Ilona was there, but I refrained since he was in good spirits.

When I went to the dressing room, my tea was waiting again, along with roses and a food menu. This time, however, there was a note with the roses. "Sorry I missed your performance. I am looking forward to hearing your beautiful voice sing for me tonight." It was signed by Ilona. My heart did a little flutter. She cared enough to make sure I was taken care of. My doubts about her were starting to feel silly.

The place was even more crowded than previous weeks. I wondered if they had heard about me or if they were there for some other reason. I straightened out my dress.

The performance went smoothly. I came out and sat at Ilona's table. I was seated right by her side as she bragged about my talent to anyone who would listen. They also talked a little business, but in vague terms and I couldn't follow. Graham sat sullenly across the table from me. He didn't say a word, but he occasionally stole a glance at me. It hurt me to look in those sad, brown eyes.

After a few minutes, Ilona leaned over and whispered in my ear. "Meet me in my office in 10 minutes."

I nodded. "I'm going to go freshen up in the dressing room. I'll see everyone later."

Her lips curved slightly up into something resembling a smile.

I touched up my make-up. I spritzed on some perfume, but I wasn't sure if vampires even cared for that sort of thing. Would she rather just smell my blood? I laughed at the silly nature of my thoughts. I glanced at my watch. It was exactly one minute until time to meet her.

I walked over to her door and knocked. There was no answer, and it felt like my heart dropped into my stomach. She snuck up behind me in the hallway while I was knocking again and put her arm around me. She pulled me towards her and caressed my face. I was speechless. Part of me wanted to protest, but all the other parts were screaming "yes!"

She gently guided me into the office. The room was full of more luxurious antique furniture. She asked me to sit on the couch and she sat as close as she could to me without sitting in my lap. My heart was racing and my mouth was dry. I couldn't think of a single damn thing to say.

This situation was completely outside of my life experience. I had never felt this way about a girl, much less a vampire. She didn't say a word, but just looked at me with a certain intensity and I thought she would bore a hole right through to my soul.

Finally, the quiet moment broke loose and she leaned in and pressed her lips to mine gently. Explosions in my head erupted as our tongues began an epic battle.

We stopped for air and she kissed down my neck and into my cleavage. In a state of bliss, I moaned. I think she took it as a sign we were headed in the right direction.

She shoved me onto my back. She took off my top and bra first, taking her time flicking her tongue over my tiny pink nipples. Then, she kissed her way down my stomach and on to my inner thighs until I was uncomfortably wet. When she finally hit the spot, I was in heaven. I orgasmed fast because of the newness and texture of it all. I was reeling.

I knew I needed to reciprocate. I tried to reach for her and grabbed her skirt. I tried to unzip it.

She gently pushed my hand away. "Another time, my lovely. You only have 25 minutes until the next show. Go rest and freshen up."

Could I even perform another show after that? I was worried when I stood up and I was shaking so bad my knees practically knocked together.

**

I had a lie down on the couch again. I sipped on some of the leftover tea before going back out for the show. It wasn't my best performance. My energy was gone, but no one seemed to notice. They all seemed just as into me as ever.

Ilona was not there, but her entourage was. I sat with them, and with the imposing Ilona gone, lots of people came to speak to me. They told me how awesome my voice was and how they'd be coming to see me again. I think a few men tried to hit on me, but I was not in my normal frame of mind so I just ignored it completely.

I was polite, but not as flirty as I normally would have been. I wondered if Ilona was the jealous type.

Either way, if she had been there, I knew they would not have dared approach me.

Graham was nowhere to be seen.

I contemplated trying to see Ilona in her office before leaving, but remembered the ominous message about never bothering her there unless invited. So I called a cab and left. Since Ilona wasn't there for the second show, I found that my insecurities were eating away at me again. I wondered if I had done something wrong.

As I drifted off to sleep that night, I thought about how her hands, lips, and tongue felt on me...so much gentler than a man. I was wet again just thinking out it. I can't remember my dreams from that night, but I'm pretty sure they were satisfying since I woke up with a smile.

***

Nothing exciting happened until Tuesday when I woke up bright and early. I went to the coffee house and waited to see if Olivia would show up. It was 10:45 a.m. before she finally arrived, but she looked genuinely happy to see me.

She came right over and sat down. "Hey! I was hoping you'd be here. I think you helped clear up my writer's block after we talked that day. I've been writing up a storm! I was even thinking about making you a character in the book."

"I'm so glad to hear that. I'd love to read it sometime...when it's done, or even sooner..."

"Let me get a few more chapters down and I will give you a hard copy to check out."

"Sounds like a deal. So what do you do for a living? Last time you said you had a meeting to go to, yet you sat here for hours..."

"I'm a legal assistant, which mostly consists of typing up forms and doing research. Most of that can be done from my laptop anywhere. My boss does need me for some cases though. He had a client meeting he wanted me there for."

"Cool."

"What do you do for a living?"

"Well…" I contemplated how to word it. "I work at a convenience store part time and I'm also a singer at a club in town."

"Oooh. That sounds more exciting than my job. What club?" She looked intrigued.

"Underland."

"I've heard of that place! It seems…interesting. Can I come hear you sing sometime? Maybe I can work this into my book somehow."

"Uh, sure. I sing Sunday nights at Midnight and 3 a.m." I considered warning her about the fact that it was a vampire club, but I didn't know if it was a good idea to betray the trust of my new employer and possibly lover. She'd have to figure it out for herself.

"Awesome. I'll try to come check you out this Sunday night."

I was happy. Now we were getting somewhere. She was willing to go out of her way to see me.

"Cool." I smiled at her.

"Listen, I don't want to be rude but I do need to get some writing done. I have got to be back to work right after lunch. We'll talk again soon, though?"

"Yeah, definitely." I got up and scooted the chair back up to the table. "See you."

I was a little sad to see the conversation end so quickly, but at least she wanted to talk again.

When I got back to the apartment, there were roses outside my door. The note read, "I hope to come see you at your home tonight if you are not working. Send word back with the messenger. Love, Ilona." I inhaled the sweet scent deeply. I had never been treated lavishly or romantically before. I couldn't remember Raphe ever getting me flowers.

I looked around anxiously for the messenger. It just so happened I was off work, but I had the feeling she knew that already. I didn't see anyone. I assumed they must have left when I wasn't home.

I set the roses on the kitchen counter. They were already in an ornate silver vase. I just kept admiring them throughout the day.

That evening, I was watching Pretty Woman on my tiny television set. It was a favorite of mine, as silly as it was. There was a knock at the door. My heart leaped. I practically bounced to the door, expecting to see Ilona there. When I opened it, Graham was standing there. "Oh. Hi, Graham."

"Don't seem so enthusiastic about it." His face was set in stone and it wasn't an attractive look for him. "Ilona wants to know if she will be allowed to come to your home tonight."

"Yes, of course. I'm not working tonight." Then there was an awkward silence. I looked past him out the door, trying to think of what I could say to him. "Look, I know you are trying to protect me. I think Ilona cares for me. I have seen proof in everything she has done. Just let me make my own decisions and I will take the consequences."

He looked me in the eyes. "Yes...she cared for them all, for a time." He turned and walked away.

I was equal parts irritated with him and also worrying about him. I considered him a friend.

6 INAMORATA

I put on a little dark red velvet dress. I put on some light make-up and waited. I paced around the apartment. It was almost 10 p.m. when there was a knock at the door. She stood in the hallway, looking at me like she was expecting something but all I could do was stare at her. She was wearing a business suit of a deep green color that brought out her eyes. I was mesmerized by her face. Her eyes shone with love and held the promise of passion.

She cleared her throat and I looked down. She was holding a little blue velvet box. I almost squealed, but I managed to hold it in for the sake of embarrassment in front of her.

"For me?"

She handed it to me and I motioned for her to come inside.

"Open it." She said softly as she hung up her suit jacket.

I opened it slowly. It was a silver necklace with a silver skeleton key on it. "I love it. Oh, thank you." I hugged her and she took it from me and put it around my neck gently. Now, you are mine."

I was not a possession. I was slightly offended and she could probably read it in my face. She spoke up. "Darling, I do not mean that I own you. I simply mean that you are my inamorata - my love. This means that no other vampire can touch you. It would be an unpardonable offense for them to do so."

I smiled at her. "I am touched by this gift."

"It is not just jewelry, my dear. It is the key to my apartment below the club. You may stay there any time you like. I am not always there, but I want you to feel welcome in my home." She glanced around my apartment. "You may keep this place too, if you like, but it doesn't seem very comfortable. My home is now yours and anything you need will be bestowed upon you, my love."

I suddenly felt ashamed of my meager apartment, but I didn't know if I was quite ready to live with her either. I was also freaking out inside. She called me "my love". Did she truly love me or was this just a term of endearment? Did I love her? I knew that I wanted desperately to be around her as much as possible.

"Thank you." I felt as though I might cry. She must have sensed my emotions bubbling to the surface because she leaned in and kissed me gently. I was just so grateful in that moment, I grabbed her face and kissed her hard. She roughly shoved me into the kitchen, against the countertop. She used her hands to pull my hips closer into her. Our legs were tangled together and I was breathing heavy. She slipped her hands up my dress and massaged my inner thighs while kissing me. I kissed her neck and ran my hands inside her suit jacket and grabbed her breasts.

It felt so strange being on the other side of being groped. She peeled off the jacket and tossed it across the room. She unbuttoned her blouse about halfway down before kissing me again, and then finishing. Frantically, the rest of the clothes flew off at an alarming rate. We headed towards the bedroom. She climbed into my bed and laid back, grinning and taking my body in with her eyes.

I climbed on top of her and kissed her nipples, and worked my way up to her mouth. She grabbed my butt with her hands and pressed me into her. The heat coming from our bodies pressed together was amazing. I hadn't known if vampires were even capable of producing heat, but this proved that they could. She tried to get up, but I pushed her back down.

I made my way back down her body with my mouth. I hungrily licked and kissed everything until I arrived at the sweet spot. I didn't know what I was doing, but she never complained. I worked her passionately into orgasm, and we held each other afterwards.

The journey was complete. I had found where I belonged - in the arms of Ilona and on the stage of Underland. I was happy. I told her about my dreams as we cuddled. She listened attentively. I fell asleep in her arms and woke up alone. That would take some getting used to. I'd be offended if I didn't know she was a vampire.

I stretched out and thought about how much I'd enjoyed talking with her, making love, and falling asleep in her arms. I did most of the talking, but she seemed to enjoy my company. I kept on thinking about her touch and how the warmth spread between us until I drifted back to sleep.

When I woke up, it was 1 p.m. I freaked out a little bit, but when I realized I was off that night I decided to relax and enjoy some down time. After all the stress I'd endured lately, I deserved it.

I got dressed and made myself some hot tea. I just sat on the couch, luxuriating in my thoughts of her. For once in the few weeks since starting at Underland, I was actually okay with just being at home. I knew where she was and that she cared for me. I was falling in love with her and I was just content with just existing in this bliss until the next time we saw each other.

I ran my fingers over the key necklace. I wondered if I could go there tonight. It wasn't that I felt that I had to see her, but the more I thought about it, the more curious I was about her apartment.

I was filled with questions. I wanted to know her history, her likes, her dislikes, and her desires. I wanted to know everything there was to know. I knew that there was more to her for me to love and I wanted to fan the flame of the love that was for now just a spark.

I flipped around to different television channels that evening, never quite settling on anything for very long. I kept spacing out and losing interest.

I wasn't sure how much time had passed while I'd just been sitting on my couch. I walked over to the window to take a quick look.

It was dark out and as I glanced down I saw Graham looking up at me, but he walked briskly away when our eyes met. He was just flat-out stalking me now. I wondered if I should bring up the subject to Ilona, but I didn't want to cause bad blood between them. I went back to the couch and tried to forget Graham and dwell on the happiness in my life.

***

The next morning, I was in such a euphoric state that I almost forgot to go to the coffee shop. I leaped out of bed rather late and prayed Olivia would still be there. She was. She waved me over when I came in the door, while still typing away on the computer. "Hey, how goes it?"

"Great, actually. Things are better than they have been in a long time."

"Excellent. May I ask what is so great, Smiley-Nina?"

"I've met someone. The job is an absolute dream. It just seems like all my ducks are in a row for once in my life."

"I'm still not over my ex from over a year ago. I've dated a few people but I find something wrong with them and kick them to the curb. Maybe something is wrong with me, but I just don't want to settle for someone at this point in my life. I want the real deal. I'd rather be alone than be with someone who doesn't truly love me."

I proceeded to tell her all about my relationship with Raphe and the former job at his club. It was like we'd only just began talking, but I glanced up and it was 1:30 p.m. "Do you have anywhere to be, Liv? It's getting kind of late."

She yelled out, "Fuck! Yes, I was supposed to be back at the office 30 minutes ago. Hopefully my boss won't notice if I slip in." She jumped up and gathered her things. "Nina, I'm hoping to come catch you perform on Sunday. Let's trade numbers so we can chat more." We quickly jotted down each other's numbers before she left.

I waved goodbye and she was already gone. I knew how to pick a friend, because I already felt like I'd known her for years. We were already at that comfort level with one another.

***

That night, I was back to the convenience store grind. I wasn't feeling very glamorous, but that was life. In the middle of the dreadful boredom, the gang of vampire thugs from my first night came to buy a few things. When I started to ring them up, a scruffy-looking fellow with dreads looked me up and down.

"You work at Underland?"

"Yes." I was a bit nervous at the question.

"They whispered amongst themselves and then the scruffy one spoke again. "You have a divine gift. You give my troubled heart peace when you sing, and for that I thank you."

I felt warm and fuzzy. It's moments like that you live for as an artist...knowing that something you have done has touched someone deeply. "You are welcome. I hope to see you again."

He nodded at me thoughtfully and they walked out. They looked at me with a high level of respect and I thought that for once my life made sense. I'd always assumed that it was my purpose in life, but this further confirmed for me that I was doing the right thing.

***

Sunday night came again. It never seemed to come soon enough. I brought some extra clothes to spend the night. By then, I was mostly over the nervousness, but I was still slightly jittery about Olivia possibly hearing me sing for the first time.

I didn't see Ilona or Graham anywhere, but Reed winked at me when I walked through on the way to the dressing room. My tea was waiting on me, but no roses that day. I knew that if I needed anything that all I had to do was ask.

I took a few moments to meditate while I was in my room. This was becoming a ritual. I'd sit on the couch or in front of the mirror and just close my eyes and breathe for a few minutes before each show. It made a world of difference in my confidence. I truly felt that I was ready to perform when I stepped on stage. I found when I closed my eyes that night, I pictured Ilona sitting in her office across the hall. I was tempted to go to her, but I knew that I shouldn't. I couldn't even be sure she was actually there.

I played with the key necklace again. Since I had a little time to kill before the show, I wondered if I could slip down to her apartment and see if she was there. If not, at least I could put my clothes down there and check it out. Trouble was, I didn't even know where it was. I walked out into the hallway and found a security guard. "Hi. Can you tell me how to get to Ilona's apartment?"

He glared at me for a moment.

"I have the key right here."

He still looked unsure. "The last door on the right over there is the stairs. When you get to the bottom of the stairs, take the hallway on the left and walk it to the end and you will see her door."

I went back to the dressing room and grabbed my tote bag with my clothes. As I walked down, I noticed that the temperature dropped even further than the frozen tundra of a hallway.

I found her apartment with no problem, but I paused at the door and listened. I couldn't hear anything behind the door or in the empty hallways at all. It was frankly a bit creepy and I considered turning back. I knocked on the door as a precaution. After a few seconds with no response, I put the key in the lock and it clicked so loudly that it echoed and frightened me just a tiny bit.

I fumbled for the light and the place was just as expected - immaculate and full of the same antique style as the rest of the place. She had wonderful taste, but it also felt very unlived-in. The place needed flowers or pictures of real people. I imagined a huge picture of us together hanging in the living room and laughed at myself.

I remembered Graham describing the apartments as small, but this one was larger than mine. Maybe hers was larger than everyone else since she was the owner. That kind of made sense. I felt like I was intruding still and called out "Ilona? Hello? You home?" There was no response.

I laid my bag down in the bedroom. I loved the king-sized canopy bed in her room with lavender fabric draping over it. I had to resist the urge to get in it and jump up and down like a giddy child. I knew I needed to get back up to the dressing room and get ready for the show, but I was tempted to snoop. I looked around intently at everything, but I didn't dare touch anything for fear she would somehow know that I messed with something. I didn't know how keen vampire sense were, but I wasn't exactly ready to find out.

I heard loud conversation coming from the hallway. I jetted out of her apartment, still feeling like I was doing something wrong, even though I had the key and the open invitation.

I found a waiter outside my dressing room holding a menu. I ordered some pasta and told him to just bring it to me at Ilona's table after the first show.

I put on my make-up and soon enough, show-time.

Ilona was seated up front again and she was beaming at me. After a few songs, I saw Liv scurry in and take a booth to my right. I smiled at her during a few numbers. When the show was done, I was torn. I wanted to run to Ilona, but I felt obligated to speak to Liv because she'd come here just to see me. I compromised. I went straight to Ilona's table. "Ilona, I have a friend who has come to see me. I am going to speak to her."

She motioned at Liv. "Her? The girl you were flirting with from the stage?"

"Oh, it isn't like that. She is a friend, but she has never heard me sing before. I just want to be polite and talk to her for a few minutes."

"Fine. Make it quick." She looked at me sternly and I was a bit intimidated.

I ran over to Liv. "What did you think?"

She looked down for a second and my heart sunk. "I loved it, doll, but this crowd sure reacts funny. They don't seem to move or get into it, but they clap for you. I don't get it. Something just doesn't feel right about this place."

My heart jumped a little. "I'll explain some other time." I told her that I was happy to see her, but I had to get back to dinner at the V.I.P. table.

I hoped she wasn't offended, but Ilona was more important to me at that time. I knew it wasn't healthy, but I was also afraid of pissing her off.

She kept me close the rest of the night, and after the second show we headed to the apartment. I was unsure anything would happen between us. I was afraid I had messed things up. She had been distant with me all night. I was aching for her attention and her touch. But as soon as we went in the apartment, all of the earlier tension disappeared.

We walked to the bedroom without a word and we stretched out on the bed together, fully-clothed. We faced each other, wordless, and she stroked my hair.

Her eyes were alight with love, and I couldn't have been happier in that moment. I'd felt lust around her constantly before, but that night we fell asleep in each other's arms and I just felt safe.

The next morning, when I looked over at her, the realization that she was a vampire set in. She looked dead while she rested, and it was chilling to see. She didn't move or breathe while she slept. Was she asleep? I still had so many questions about vampires, but I didn't know if asking so many questions would be annoying to them. I made a mental note to ask Graham a few more questions next time I saw him.

Thinking of Graham upset me. I knew that he was hurting and I was at fault. I wondered if we were still going to be able to maintain a friendship. I hoped for it.

I wasn't sure how many hours left there were of daylight, but I couldn't just stay in the bedroom with her looking dead. Plus it was so quiet in the apartment that I thought I might lose my mind if I stayed in there for hours. I changed into comfy clothes and headed up to the bar. I knew it wasn't open, but I decided to explore. I ended up going straight to the kitchen and pilfered some food to make a club sandwich. After I was satisfied, I played around on the stage. I sang a little bit, and felt a thrill at the acoustics of the empty room. I was even brave enough to try her office, but it was locked. Immediately after trying, I was a little ashamed that I would even do such a thing. I was relieved that it was locked. Maybe there were things that I didn't want to know. Plus I knew that angering her would be a really bad thing.

I got bored with the deserted bar fast. I decided to venture out. When I stepped outside, I realized there were guards outside. They looked at me strangely when I came out the door. I think I startled them. "Not used to seeing anyone come out in daylight, are ya?" They chuckled.

As I got around the corner from the club, I called Liv. I got her voicemail and left a message. I stood in the street for a minute. I didn't know what to do. I had no plans until work at the convenience store later that night. I didn't know many places to go in the area, but I didn't want to go back to the club or my own apartment.

***

I wandered so many blocks that I lost count. My feet were tired so I wanted into a little 50's diner called The

Greasy Jukebox. It was small, but had an anachronistic charm. The smell of old burger grease hit me like a truck when I walked in. I sat and ordered a large breakfast even though it was afternoon. I had waffles, eggs, bacon, and toast. It was an indulgence I rarely enjoyed, but it was worth it.

The time alone to think and eat was beneficial to my soul. I loved Ilona, but the more I thought about it, the more I realized how little I knew of her. I had to get to know her better and stop being afraid of her. I knew that fear in a relationship was dangerous. I spent the last few months of my relationship with Raphe in constant fear of him firing me, but I knew that the thing was doomed. It was a waste of time. I was miserable. But with Ilona, I wanted to work on it and make things better. I didn't feel like doing anything with her was a waste of time. I was convinced she was my one and only.

I was feeling rejuvenated, so I headed back to the club to goof around. I performed a silly little dance routine on the stage. I tried my hand at mixing fancy cocktails, but mostly those turned out awful and they ended up in the trash. I even tried to find out what was in the other rooms in the hallway, but my snooping was unsuccessful. Most of the doors were locked.

When it was almost dark, I slipped back into bed. I wanted to be there when she awoke. I watched her for what seemed like an eternity. I memorized the porcelain skin and every curve and line of her that I could see. I started caressing her silken hair when her eyes opened abruptly and it startled me a little bit. She grabbed my face and kissed me. "I'm so happy you stayed, my lovely."

"Why wouldn't I? You've made it so welcoming here for me." I grinned at her.

"Well, I'm glad. I had the most wonderful dream about you singing on the stage and the whole club was empty. It was so blissful that I had the most restful sleep I've had in a long time."

"Oh." I found it odd that she would dream this and I guess she could read the thought on my face.

"Something wrong, love.?" She looked worried.

"I...went upstairs and I actually did sing on the stage while you were sleeping."

She laughed. "Well, that's a fun coincidence, dear.

Don't think on it too hard."

"So you don't have some kind of weird vampiric super-sonic hearing or something?"

"Ha! No. Some vampires have certain gifts, but they are small and not super-hero powers. That would be quite silly."

"I see." I suddenly felt a bit stupid. She'd probably been around for centuries and here I was asking about super-powers. Oh, silly, silly Nina. I had hoped to ask more vampire questions, but I thought that might be my quota for the night.

Suddenly one strange thing occurred to me. She had never asked to drink my blood. Since I was asking stupid things, I thought, well, one more won't hurt, right? "Ilona, why have you never drank my blood? You need that to survive, right?"

"Darling, I have many willing donors. Some vampires who are younger or less attractive may have to ask, but I never have. Donors and lovers have always offered themselves to me." She ran her fingers through my hair and continued. "Vampires can go years without drinking blood, but it makes them weaker. There are a few out there who try to do without. It's a very difficult life. Very monk-like. They survive, but I'm not sure how enjoyable or functional that life is."

"Wow. Do you know any vampires like that?"

"Not that extreme, but Graham goes for long lengths of time without, and he never drinks directly from a donor. He drinks blood from a wine glass when he feels he needs the boost. It's not the same. I don't know how he does it." She shook her head disapprovingly.

"How is that not the same?" I was perplexed.

She laughed. "I heard a saying once that compared sex to pizza. Sometimes sex is like microwave pizza. It's still pizza and you may enjoy it, but it's not good pizza. I believe the same applies here. You see, when you pour it in a cup, it loses warmth and flavor; it's less fresh. Just not the same."

"Ah, gotcha." I was thinking a million more questions, but she grabbed my hips and pulled me closer. What were those darn questions again? Oh. My. God.

She slowly removed my jeans and blouse. She caressed and kissed my inner thighs for what seemed like ages and I wanted to scream for her to please make love to me when she rubbed her body against mine while laying a lingering kiss on me. I stopped her abruptly mid-kiss. "You can drink from me. I love you. I would rather you drank from me than someone else."

She suddenly looked at me with an intense hunger in her eyes. She gently took my hand and caressed my arm. I looked away and it felt like she was kissing my arm for a long time. I was in ecstasy. I was wondering when she was going to actually bite me, but when I looked up she was licking her lips. Then she headed towards my breasts and teased my nipples with her tongue.

We took things slow this time. We kissed and caressed each other everywhere and took turns licking each other. I'm not sure how much time passed and I didn't care. Time had stopped while we explored each other intimately and comfortably. The other times we had frantically had sex. This time we had made love.

When it was over and I lay there, I asked her if she had bitten me.

"Yes. Of course. You asked me to."

"I didn't even feel it…"

"I'm gentle with my lovers. I'm not as careful with people I don't care about." She shot me a frightening grin.

I would hate to be a person she didn't care about. "I love you."

She ran her hand up my thigh. "I love you, as well. Now get ready for your mundane job. It's getting late and I have my own business to attend also."

I was a little hurt by that, but it was true and I couldn't argue. I put on my clothes.

"Darling, will you be back after work?" she queried.

"I don't get off until the morning so there's no point. I was thinking I'd just come here on the nights I don't work, if that's okay?"

"Whatever you are comfortable with. If you wish to leave that job, you know I can easily give you a raise."

"I don't think that's necessary." I blushed. I didn't like the job, but I felt weird about accepting a raise for no reason.

We both got ready in the bathroom, barely speaking. We kissed and went our separate ways for the evening. I was walking on air.

7 BITTEN BY THE LOVE BUG

Monday night at work was boring, but I didn't mind because I was so damned happy. Happiness was fleeting and I was wise enough to enjoy it while it was visiting me. I found that I was spaced-out most of the night and the customers had to snap me out of it at times by shouting at me from across the counter. It was ridiculous, but I didn't care.

Tuesday, I went to the coffee shop, but Liv wasn't there. I waited until lunch and probably drank enough coffee to kill a horse. I was sad and worried she was angry at me after the way I abandoned her at the show. I'd hoped she would understand once I explained, but now I wasn't sure that was going to happen. I was losing friends like crazy.

In a dreadful mood, I walked back to my apartment. Just as I was getting to my building, my cell phone rang.

"Hey, it's Liv. I'm sorry I never got back to you. It's been hectic at work. I can't come to the coffee shop today, but I wanted to see if you wanted to meet somewhere later for dinner or drinks or whatever?"

"Sure. What time?" I was trying to hold in how giddy I was that we were still cool. If she had been there I'm not sure I could've resisted the urge to hug her and jump up and down like we just won the lottery.

"Is 6:30 good? Where ya wanna go?"

I was silent for a moment. I couldn't think of anywhere except... "6:30 is good. Hey, there's a 50's diner over on Turner St. I tried the other day. Do you like greasy food?"

"Honey, have you met me? Of course I love greasy food."

I laughed. "Okay, see you at 6:30. I think it's called...Jukebox something or other. You can't miss it."

"Okay. See you then!"

***

I went upstairs and did some cleaning and laundry at my apartment. I packed a few things since I was off. I was usually off Tuesdays and Wednesdays at the store, but that was always subject to change. I assumed I'd be staying at the club until Thursday morning. I wanted to be sure I had everything I'd need.

I called a cab at about 5 p.m. to make sure that it got there in plenty of time. I didn't want to be late for seeing my wonderful new friend.

I ended up arriving at 6:05 p.m. but I went ahead and got a booth since it was crowded. She showed up around 6:20. She was wearing a nice grey business suit. It was slimming on her.

"You're looking wonderful." I smiled at her.

She laughed. "I think maybe it's because I'm spending less time eating in my spare time and more time actually writing. I think you've become my muse. Writing never went so smoothly before I met you."

We both had burgers and fries, but I splurged and got a shake. I couldn't get enough of the food. I knew it was bad for me, but it was comforting as well. While we ate, I tried to tactfully get her caught up on what had been going on.

"Well, okay, you know how you were saying you thought the club crowd was a little weird?" I waited. I had been thinking and rethinking how to approach the subject carefully. I knew I had to have someone to talk about it with.

"Yes, they were. It was enough to give me the creeps." She raised an eyebrow and waited cautiously.

Then I just started rambling. "Um...I hope to God this doesn't freak you out, but they are....well, vampires. Not all of them, but some of them and I'm not even sure which ones myself. They are not all scary. Some are quite nice. So umm...there it is." I finally took a breath.

Her eyes got really wide, but she seemed to process it quickly. "Okay. I guess I've always heard there were vampires out there, but it's not something you really think about seriously, you know? You just think...yeah there's probably some crazy dudes with a blood-sucking fetish, but you don't think there are real, honest-to-God vampires."

"They've been good to me there. It's the best job I've ever had. They are really not bad. I mean, I'm sure there are bad ones, but so far I haven't met any."

"Cool. I guess I'm okay with it. I mean I was there and no one attacked me or sucked my blood." She still looked a bit skeptical, but I was glad she was being so calm about it.

"Yeah, they aren't really allowed to do that."

"So nobody has sucked your blood yet, Nina?" She teased in a joking tone.

"Oh...well." I blushed.

"Oh my God. I was just kidding, but you have actually been bitten? What happened?" She appeared to be a little shocked.

"Well, I'm kind of seeing the owner of the club,

Ilona. I offered myself to her. It was actually quite pleasant. It didn't feel dangerous at all."

"You're seeing a woman and she's a vampire. This is certainly news! Details, please!"

"She's the lovely lady with black hair at the V.I.P. table. I never considered a relationship with a woman before, but she was charming and beautiful and powerful. I found her irresistible."

"Wowzers. I just can't get over this. You really know how to throw someone a curve-ball, lady." She just sat sipping her soda and shaking her head.

"I know. It's still a shock for me. I don't know vampire etiquette or even that much about them in general, but I'm learning. I know that we're in love and I'm happy."

"Well, I'm glad then. You look happy. I've got to find me someone. I need a hunky vampire. Maybe you can introduce me to someone?"

I laughed. "I don't know but a few of them, but I'll see about it."

She sighed. "I'm halfway kidding, but if I met the right one I might be into it. I'm just desperate right now. I'm trying to get over Fenn."

"Your ex?"

"No...Fenn is a lawyer at the firm I work for, but I work for one of the other lawyers. I don't see him often, but he is beautiful. I've had a crush on him since I've worked there, but he doesn't know I exist, of course. Every attempt I've made to get his attention has been disastrous."

"Oh well, you will find someone who will shower you with attention. You're a lovely girl."

"Are you hitting on me, Nina?" She laughed and I joined in. "I'm happy we have become friends, Miss Muse." She got up and paid for our meal. I thanked her and headed out to walk to the club.

I regretted my decision to wear heels. When I arrived, I glanced around to see if I could spot anyone I knew. I was disappointed in that endeavor. I went to the hallway guard and asked if Ilona was in. He shrugged. "I think she's out, but who knows?" He wasn't exactly helpful.

I went back out into the bar and sat down at a booth. Within seconds Reed made his way over to me. It was a relief to see a familiar face. "What do you need tonight, Nina?"

"I'll have a water and a drink menu, Reed. Oh and do you know if Ilona is here tonight?"

"Nope. She sure isn't. Was she expecting you?"

"I guess not." I was disappointed.

After I finished off the ice water, I ordered a succession of various alcoholic beverages. After I'd sat there for a while, Reed came by and asked if I was okay. "I'm fine. Hey, Reed, I haven't seen Graham lately. Do you know where he's been?"

"The Mistress sent him on a mission to a foreign country. No one knows exactly where or what he's doing."

I found myself even sadder about this than one would've expected. I liked talking to him. He was a very good listener and he had kind eyes. I wanted to see him again. I hoped he would return soon. "Okay, when he comes back or you know, if he calls or something, could you tell him I need to talk to him?"

"Sure thing, Nina. I'll get word to him." He winked at me. I left him an excellent tip and then let myself into Ilona's apartment and passed out.

As far as I could tell, she never came home that night. If she did, she wasn't there when I woke up the next morning. I was a little hurt, but I had no idea what kind of business she dealt with so I couldn't be angry with her until I knew what was going on.

I only spent a few minutes in the apartment before deciding to just go home. I couldn't stand quiet, the loneliness, or the lack of entertainment. I grabbed my things and called a cab.

I didn't hear from her on Wednesday either. Thursday, I went to the coffee shop and talked to Liv. I shared my frustration with her.

"I can't believe she hasn't even contacted me in days. I'm feeling ripped-open. I don't know how to communicate this." I let out an exasperated sigh. "I know she's busy doing whatever it is she does, but I need to know she's going to be there for me." I felt vulnerable and irritated, and I knew it was a little selfish of me to put my expectations on her. I guess this was the part where the newness of the relationship started to wear off. It seemed too soon for that.

"Sounds to me like you're just feeling left out. Why don't you just ask her what's going on and try to find a way to fit yourself into her life more."

"I guess that makes sense. I don't even know where to start with her. She's very intimidating at times."

"Every relationship needs honesty. Just be honest and demand the same from her. That's all you need. If she can't handle that, you don't need to be together."

I nodded. "You are good at this."

She laughed. "Maybe not, since I can't seem to find someone."

"Come to the club sometime and maybe you'll meet someone. Couldn't hurt."

"Ha. Maybe I'll come watch you sing again Sunday. If I don't meet someone, at least I'll be entertained."

"It's a date."

We made a little more small talk and then I left.

***

The next few days I was miserable. There was no contact from Ilona, and I was going through extreme mood swings. Sometimes I was still happy about being in love. Other times I was sad and hurt at being away from her. And a big part of me grew more and more angry because I felt I had been duped and she really didn't care that much about me.

I resisted the urge to go there. I even considered calling in sick to the convenience store so I could go run to her, but I felt a bit disgusted at myself for considering this. I suffered in silence.

Saturday after work, Kal was waiting for me outside. He was pacing at the corner when I came out the door. I was happy to see him, but as soon as I saw his face I knew something was amiss.

"What's up, Kal? Is something wrong?"

"You shouldn't go home, Nina. Raphe found out

you were working at that other club. He has some thugs waiting for you outside your apartment to bring you to him for a 'talk'." He glanced up at the sky for a moment and then he turned back to me looking stern. "You should avoid your apartment for a while until he calms down. Do you have somewhere else to stay?"

"Yes, Kal. I do. Thanks for telling me." He offered me a ride so I had him take me to the club. On the ride, we talked some more. "How did he find out, Kal? You didn't tell him, did you?"

"No. Some customer casually mentioned that he had seen you sing at Underland. He flipped his shit. Business is not good right now and none of the girls seem to want him anymore either. He used to have a way with the ladies and now they kinda see him as used-up."

"Or they are seeing him for the Grade-A douchebag he really is." I gave him a reassuring smile. "Anyway, thanks for letting me know. I can't avoid my apartment forever, though. Do you think I could just get him to talk about this?"

"Not at the moment. He is furious."

"He doesn't own me. He fired me. Now I have a better gig and he's just angry he isn't getting a piece of the action." I made a fist subconsciously and my fingernails started digging into my palm.

"That's true, but part of him still loves you too. I know that doesn't excuse the behavior, but he does."

"Does he know how much danger he is in if he comes up to Underland?"

"You mean does he know it's full of vamps? No. He doesn't want to bring it there yet. He does know there's going to be security there and he's not completely stupid. I have a feeling if he realizes he can't get you at your apartment, he may try."

"Do you think he would try to hurt me, Kal?"

"I don't think he truly intends to, but if you turn him down again on coming back...well, things might turn ugly. You know how his temper is."

I kissed Kal on the cheek and hurriedly told him goodbye and thanks again. It was daybreak so the club was empty. I let myself into the apartment quietly and creeped into the bedroom.

***

Ilona was resting and she didn't move. She was there and she still hadn't contacted me. I decided that I'd just wait and find out what happened before I got angry.

I snuggled up with her. I felt safe there. She would never let Raphe get to me. After a few minutes, I drifted off to sleep.

I woke up mid-afternoon and of course she was still resting. I got up and wandered down to the club and made a sandwich. I was thinking about investing in some books if I was going to keep getting stuck at the club. There were no radios or televisions to be seen. I assumed there was a computer somewhere but I wasn't sure where I was allowed. I eventually got bored and slipped back into bed with Ilona to sleep longer.

She shook me lightly to wake me up. She seemed very happy to see me. "Where have you been, love? I had to go for a little trip, but I expected you here upon my return."

"I had to work my mundane job and I didn't know when you'd be back from your...trip."

"I sense annoyance in your voice. Confess to me what is bothering you." She appeared to be genuinely concerned.

I turned away from her slightly. "I guess I just feel left out of your life. You never tell me where you are going or what you are doing. You just disappear. I feel like this is only a relationship when it's convenient for you."

"Vampire business is secretive. I have to check up on rogue vampires and also discipline law-breakers in this area because I'm the oldest in this region. That's about as much as I can tell you. To tell you more would only put you in danger. If you are not satisfied with that, we can surely end this."

The flash of fire in her eyes was enough to shut me up. I sat silent for a few moments.

Her voice and demeanor began to soften. "And furthermore, I have the club and other businesses along the coast that keep me busy. It's time consuming, but just know that I'd rather be with you."

She wrapped an arm around me and I recoiled just a little. "Darling, you need not fear me. I love you. I will try to be better about letting you know when I will be gone. It may not come from my own lips, but I will leave word." She caressed my shoulders lovingly. "Also, if you wish, you can come with me when it's not vampire business. Would that make you happy?" It seemed as though she was talking down to me.

"That's...not necessary." Suddenly, I was overcome with stress and emotion. I started sobbing.

She patiently held me until I calmed. My other worries spilled out. "Raphe has found out I'm working here and has sent some people to wait for me at my apartment. I came here for your protection. I'm afraid of what he might do."

She laughed softly and my heart felt eased. "I will not let him harm you. He will not win you back as his lover or even his worker. Stay here and be safe."

"All of my things are at my apartment...I can't go get them."

She smiled and held my chin up to look at her. "I

will send some of my people there tonight to go fetch your things. Do not worry. Everything will be fine."

We kissed and yet again I remembered why I loved her. She was so good to me.

My performances went well. I clung to her side while she mingled at the club. I even followed her to her office while she made some calls. When we retired back to her apartment, most of my belongings lay in a neat pile of boxes in her living room and bedroom. Things in my life were changing fast, and I wasn't sure I was ready. I sat down on the couch, feeling overwhelmed. She sensed it and she sat down beside me. "What's the problem?"

"Staying over here sometimes is fun, but I'm not sure I was ready to actually live together."

"It's temporary for your own protection."

"I know…"

"I'll tell you what…spend the night with me and if you decide you aren't comfortable with it, I have another empty apartment that you can use here at the club."

"Thank you." A wave of relief came over me. We hugged and that turned into caressing, which of course, turned into us making love on the couch.

The next day, I decided to give the living arrangement a try. I decided to keep my apartment at least until I figured out what to do with my furniture. It was official. I was a lady vampire's live-in girlfriend. How surreal!

I didn't know what to do with myself, but at least I had my television and some books! I set up the television on the coffee table temporarily.

I called up Maurice and told him that I wouldn't be in and didn't know if I could come back since I was in danger. He told me that I'd have a job if I ever did decide to come back. I knew I was putting him in a bind, but I knew that Raphe's men would probably look for me there.

I ventured out for groceries to stock the barren refrigerator. I called Liv while I was out. "Hi, doll," she answered sweetly.

"I've moved in with Ilona."

"Wow. That was fast. Uh. I'm happy for you I guess?"

"It was a bit of a necessity. Psycho ex-boyfriend is trying to get me back or something. I'm hiding out at Ilona's place."

"Does he know where you're at?"

"I don't think so, but since he's had someone follow me before, it's possible."

"That's terrible, but maybe you'll be safe with Ilona. By the way, sorry I didn't know up Sunday night. Work stuff took over my life again. I will come soon, I promise. We just have a really high profile case right now."

"It's okay. I don't want to hurt your feelings, but with so much going on, I kinda forgot you were even coming!"

"Wow, that IS bad." She giggled. "Well, I'm going to let you go. My boss will return from court any second and I don't want to get caught on a personal call. Good to hear from you, though. I promise I'll come to the club for a visit soon."

"Thanks for listening." I really cared for Liv. She did wonders for my sanity.

***

For a few weeks I lived a blissful existence. I was almost domestic. I cleaned and stayed close to the club. I was always patiently waiting for Ilona. We made love every chance we got. I hadn't heard anything out of Raphe or his men. There was no word from Graham, either. I talked to Liv by phone from time to time, but I didn't yet venture out to the coffee shop. So my whole world was Ilona and Liv. It was limiting, but they were my people and I loved them.

Finally, Liv came by a few Sundays after the move. She came early and I saw her hanging around the bar. I had her come sit at a booth with me.

Reed took our drink and food orders. I could tell that Liv was intrigued by him. As soon as he walked away, she leaned in and whispered, "Is he, you know, one of them?"

"Reed? Umm...I don't think so. I have never seen

him outside the club so I can't be sure, but most of the workers are humans, I believe. So, it stands to reason that he would be human."

"Either way, he's yummy. Introduce us?"

"Sure." I grinned.

When he came back, I introduced them. He grinned at her. Maybe we had a match. I couldn't be sure.

After my first show, I saw her chatting with him at the booth. He was sitting with her so I left them alone.

Ilona wasn't around. I was a little relieved because it gave me a chance to mingle without her glaring eye. Before I went on for the second show, Liv came and found me at the bar and informed me in an excited high-pitched screech that she and Reed traded numbers and were meeting for coffee later in the week. I hugged her and told her I was happy for her. She told me it was getting too late for her and waved goodbye as she left the bar.

I performed my second show and made the rounds to speak to random audience members to soak up their praise. When I headed for the for the apartment, I grew bold and knocked on Ilona's office door. She beckoned me to enter. She glared at me and closed a laptop. I was shocked because it was the first time I'd seen a computer in the place!

"Is this important, dear? I'm in the middle of something."

"No, I just...I was heading to bed for the night and I wanted to see you."

"How...sweet." She rose from the desk and gave me a quick kiss on the lips. Then she opened the door for me. "You know I love you, but please don't disturb me in the office unless it is an emergency. I thought this was made clear, but if it was not, then you should know now." I swallowed hard. "Yeah. See you later."

"Perhaps."

I went to bed alone and woke up alone. Was I really in a relationship?

8 LONELY HEARTS CLUB

Thursday afternoon, I received an excited call from Liv, detailing her coffee date with Reed. They'd really hit it off and she was very glad to have someone to tell about it.

"He's so beautiful. I can't believe he seems into me. It's like I'm going to wake up from a dream any moment now. Thank you, thank you, thank you for introducing me to him!"

"Glad to have helped out with McDreamypants." We both laughed.

"How's your life with MISS Dreamypants?"

"Wonderful, but I am getting a little cabin fever."

"Well, let's meet up soon. I'll probably need to talk about my date with Reed."

"When's that?"

"Tomorrow night! He's taking me to a play called 'The Secret of Touch' before his shift at the club."

"Ooh! I've heard that play is good. Let me know how it is. I might want to see it."

"Any excuse to get out of vampire prison, right?"

"I'm not in prison. Ilona's protecting me." My jaw tightened with the implication.

"I know, dear. I'll call you to set up a gossip date, okay?"

***

Saturday afternoon, Liv called and asked me to meet her at the diner for a late lunch. I was more than happy to go after the boredom of the last three days.

She was positively glowing. I could see her beam of happiness shining across the room as soon as I walked into the diner.

"The play was good, but afterwards we went to his place and wow. Just wow."

"You had sex with him on the first date?" Not that I could really talk. Ilona and I hadn't yet had an official date.

"It wasn't the first date if you count the coffee shop."

"Right." I cleared my throat.

"The play was about vampire lovers. Isn't that funny? Apparently, Reed's very into vampires. He says he's only dated vampires for the past few years, but he says I'm a breath of fresh air."

"I guess that explains why he works in a vampire club." I started to regret my part in the two of them getting together. I had no idea that Reed had a thing for vampires. That complicated things. I hoped he wouldn't hurt her.

"He's a sweetheart though. He opens doors for me. He brought me flowers. He dresses in only the finest clothes when we go out. It almost shames me to be seen with him because he's always dressed better than me."

"Sounds wonderful." I started to feel ashamed of my own relationship. There they were again. The doubts. I thought about how little I got to see her. How little I actually knew her. I looked at Liv, positively glowing, and wished for what she had.

We both ordered a bunch of junk we didn't need to eat, and knew we'd regret it later. Liv continued to gush on about every little detail about her and Reed's date.

I was feeling jealous. It was not because I wanted Liv or Reed, though Reed was a handsome guy. I wanted normalcy. I felt like the newness in my relationship with Ilona had worn off too quickly. I was already feeling like I'd been chewed up and spit out. I was feeling taken for granted. How in the world could I live like this?

I tried to feign interest in Liv's bubbly spewing, but

I just smiled and nodded, occasionally throwing in a "yep" or an "okay". She didn't seem to notice that something else was going on with me. Perhaps I should've looked into being an actress.

I needed to feel wanted and I was craving the attention that Ilona had given to me when we first met. Now I felt like a possession, another elegant bauble for her collection. She didn't deem it necessary to give me any more attention than she found convenient for her own devices.

We wrapped up our little meeting with a hug, and I headed back to the club. I enjoyed the walk back. I could have gotten someone to drive me, but I needed that walk to clear my head.

***

I snuck into the apartment and peeked in on Ilona. I climbed into bed with her when it came close to time for her awakening. Studying her beauty was one of my favorite pastimes, but that evening I wasn't sure I could ignore the issues we were having.

When she awoke, she climbed atop me and held me down. She licked me and bit me and we made love.

Afterwards, she dressed quickly to leave and as she headed out the door, she glanced back. "Perhaps you should try a diet or some exercise. You seem to have put on some weight."

I was speechless as she walked out the door. Did my lover just call me fat? I studied myself in the mirror. I found there was a little bit of extra pudge but nothing major. Did I have to lose weight to keep her? I was more than a little insulted, but I wasn't sure what to do about it.

I showered and primped in an effort to cheer myself up. I made the rounds and flirted with everyone in the place. I'd show her! Many men bought me drinks and talked me up, but quickly lost interest. I finally ended up at the bar.

A man who had been sitting at the other end of the bar moved down to sit by me. He was olive-skinned with long, dark hair pulled back into a ponytail. He leaned in towards me. "Out to prove something?"

"Is it that obvious?" I sipped my wine.

He chuckled. "You look lovely. Let's get a booth together so we can talk more privately."

I glanced around and didn't see Ilona anywhere. She was probably holed-up in her office and I would most likely not see her the rest of the night.

"Sure." I hopped off my barstool and followed him to a corner booth. I had a seat, and he ordered me some more wine.

"I'm Leland. I've seen you sing a few times. You're Ilona's inamorata, Nina, aren't you?"

"Yes."

"I'm not a fan of Ilona. She's a controlling, evil woman." He gauged my reaction to this. I tried to control my emotions and keep a straight face, but I was floored. I would have gotten up and walked away right then, but I was curious about what he had to say.

"I'm sorry if this offends you, but I'm a friend of her daughter, Zaleska. She has her kind moments, but she is a very selfish person. You will learn this with time."

"I didn't know she had a daughter." I felt my heart sink. "She's been very kind to me. I don't know what to say." I looked around nervously. I wanted to know more, but I couldn't bring myself to ask more. I was scared she could have a way of listening.

He continued anyway. "Her daughter is like Snow White. Ilona is like the evil queen. Ilona made her daughter into a vampire to keep her young and beautiful forever. Her daughter did not want it. She forced it on her. She hates Ilona for it, but there isn't much she can do. Ilona is powerful and feared."

"Where does Zaleska live?"

"She travels around, but mostly in Europe and Asia. She avoids America the majority of the time because of her mother."

"Where's the father?" I asked while also pondering who he might be.

"He is not around." He looked around nervously.

"I have a question." I leaned in and whispered, "I've heard that Ilona kills her mates when she tires of them. Is this true?"

"I have not witnessed it, but I have heard the same bit of information."

"I can't imagine it to be true. She does love me. She may not have as much time for me as I'd like, but she takes care of me."

"People take care of pets, but it doesn't mean they will keep them forever."

There was no use arguing. I didn't know this man. Why was I even listening to him? "Thank you for the drink, sir," I said.

I stood up to leave and he grabbed my arm. "Meet me in front of the bank around the corner in about 15 minutes. I need to speak to you more privately."

"I don't know that I can trust you."

He looked around again. "Graham sent me."

My heart stopped for a moment. I nodded. "Ok," I whispered.

I went to the dressing room and sat on the couch for a few minutes to gather my wits. I was feeling the effects of the alcohol and from the shock of hearing all these things at once. I didn't know this man and didn't trust him, but I knew I had to hear him out if he was a messenger from Graham.

I tried to act nonchalant as I walked out of the club. When I rounded the corner, I didn't see the man anywhere. I started to feel frightened.

He stepped out of the shadows of the overhang in front of the bank. He walked up to me slowly. "No one followed you?"

I glanced back. "Not that I know of."

He glanced around me. "Graham got your message and asked that you come to him. He wants to speak to you about everything that has happened."

"I can't just up and leave."

"He thought you should know that she sent him out of the country because of you."

"Because of me?" I was perplexed.

"Because he tried to interfere with her intent to 'woo' you."

"Why would he do that?"

"For your own protection."

"I guess I can see that. I understand why he would think I need protection, but I am perfectly capable of making my own decisions and I feel perfectly safe."

He looked grim. "Well, I've delivered the message as I was told. Graham wants to speak to you in person. If you won't come to him, he'll probably come to you and put himself in danger by defying her. Just think it over, will you?"

"No. Besides the obvious reasons why I can't go drop everything and go to Europe, I also don't even have a passport."

"I will tell Graham all that you have said. I hope you will remain safe. You seem very like Zaleska, oddly. Maybe this is why Graham loves you."

"Graham...loves me? He doesn't even know me."

"He knows you far better than you are able to comprehend."

"I've got to get back…"

"Before she notices you are gone?" He gave me a smirk, confident in his knowledge.

He knew that I was nervous of angering her and that made me feel defiant. "I don't care about that."

He nodded. "Yet again, be safe." And then he disappeared into the shadows again.

I walked slowly back to the club. I walked in and sat back down at the booth to digest what was said. I'd only been seated for seconds when one of the hall guards came up to me. "The mistress wishes to see you."

"Okay, tell her I'll be there in a moment. Is she in her office?"

"She's in her office, but she demands to see you now."

Uh-oh. My pulse quickened. I followed him down the hallway, and he stayed behind while I entered her office. She stood up from her desk, but she did not look at me directly. She looked down at the floor. She walked towards me and stopped about two feet in front of me. She quickly shot her hand out and grabbed my chin and pulled my face closer to hers. "Who is the man you've been talking to half the night?"

I swallowed. "Just a guy named Leland. He said he'd seen me sing. He paid me compliments and bought me wine. There was nothing going on...just harmless flirtations."

She reached up and grabbed a lock of my wild hair and pulled me even closer. "Do not do this again. You are my inamorata and you may not behave this way. My employees watch you. I know what you do. They told me of you sitting with him and drinking. Then you disappeared for a while. You enjoyed yourself too much tonight. Go to the apartment and wait for me there. We will talk more of this later when I am less angry." She let go of my hair and turned away. My heart dropped into my stomach.

I almost broke out in a sob from the coldness she showed me in that moment. I turned and sprinted to the apartment. I wanted to run out the door of the club and never look back, but I didn't feel that was an option right now. What other choice did I have? Home wasn't safe. Raphe would have guys waiting for me there. And now this.

I was angry and upset at myself for getting caught up in this situation. And yet I still loved her. I feared her just as much as I had feared Raphe. Why did I seek these relationships instead of healthy ones? I slammed the door of the apartment behind me and ran to the bathroom. I sat down in the tub and turned the shower on. I cried and let the hot water run over my body.

***

After I was done with my emotional outburst, I anxiously paced around the apartment. I was scared, but mostly I was worried that I wouldn't have the courage to walk away. I knew that it was what I should do, but I loved her and I didn't know where to go. I'd spent the time we were together picturing how perfect our life would be together, and never once did it live up to my expectations - except in bed. That did not constitute a relationship. I was more like a sexual pet. I sat on the couch and just waited.

When she came through the door, I got up to greet her, but immediately sat back down. She was a vision of loveliness and she had obviously calmed. She came and sat beside me. She slid her arm around me.

"Darling, I'm sorry for the way I acted earlier. You must understand that I am not human. We handle things differently. I do not mean to hurt you. I just don't want to lose you."

I felt my resolve slip and fought for strength. "You scare me, Ilona. I don't know how I feel about that."

She held me tightly and kissed me on the forehead. "I certainly don't mean to scare you. I truly love you. You are special to me."

I pulled away. "I need some time to think."

There was a quick flash of anger in her eyes, but she held back. "Okay." She got up and walked into the bedroom and closed the door behind her.

I was left sitting there, stunned. I grabbed my purse and cell phone and walked out. I called Liv on the way out.

Once I hit the street, I let out a gasp of relief. Liv assured me I could stay a few days at her place. Thank goodness I had become friends with her. I don't know if anyone else would have opened their home to me so easily. She sat up with me to talk.

"She is just so damn scary. I don't know whether she harmed her other girlfriends or boyfriends or whatever, but now I feel she is capable. Do you think it would be stupid for me to hang around with this knowledge?"

"Well...yeah, honestly." She looked apologetic for what she had said.

"But, I love her. As dumb and misguided as it is, I do love her. I'm scared to leave. I'm scared to stay. What the hell do I do?" I collapsed onto her shoulder and sobbed until I was out of tears and energy.

She stroked my hair and told me it was going to be okay. I honestly don't think she really had a piece of advice for this situation, but bless her, she tried to help anyway.

***

I was wiping the mascara streaks from my face when there was a knock at the door. She went to answer it and came back with Reed. "Dear, Reed has some worrisome news."

"Okay?"

Reed sat down next to me. "Ilona has some of her vamps out looking for you. She's angry that she doesn't know where you're at and she suspects you won't be back. She's demanded that you be brought to her."

I stood up. "Is that why you're here? To take me to her?"

"No! I'm here to warn you because it's only a matter of time before she traces you here."

My heart raced. "We've got to find somewhere to go. I have a little bit of money saved from working at the club. I can get a hotel for a few days or something...Where should we go?"

Liv's face froze, deep in thought. Then she jumped up. "Let me go make a phone call..."

Reed and I just sat in silence while Liv went to her bedroom and closed the door.

When she came out 20 minutes later, she had some

bags in hand. "I've called my grandparents in New Hampshire. They have an old farmhouse there. We are welcome to stay as long as we like. I told them you were having some problems with an ex, but didn't elaborate."

"I don't even have clothes."

"We can find a thrift store or something along the way and pick up a few things." She put down her bags and gave a slight smile. "It will be okay. I have to call my boss in the morning though and explain why I'm taking my vacation days without any warning. Now, that will be a feat."

Reed spoke up. "I can't go. It'll look suspicious. I'll call and update you if I hear anything at work."

Liv nodded in agreement. I caught his eye and mouthed "thank you".

I sighed and then there was an awkward silence until I spoke up. "Let's go." Despite the situation I was in, I was actually looking forward to the trip.

I let Reed and Liv have a few moments while I took a nap. It was already morning and past time to get out of town.

9 NANA'S BANANA CREAM PIE

We had fun stopping at funky little thrift and consignment shops along the way. We picked up some hideous canary-yellow luggage to put my "new" things in. We laughed and talked about high school boyfriends and other childhood misadventures. We sang along to some 70's classic rock on the radio. I had so much fun on the way, I almost forgot that this trip was really to escape all the danger in my life.

When we pulled up to the farmhouse, I was taken aback at how gorgeous it was. The house itself was a little run-down, but the property was breath-taking. To the left of the house was a field with a small pond and to the right was a wooded area that wrapped around the back.

When we got out and walked to the door, we were met on the front porch by a rambunctious sheep dog, whom Liv introduced to me. His name was Bert. Liv's grandmother opened the door for us and then yelled, "Herb! Come get the girls' bags." She turned to us and said, "Come in, dears. Don't worry about those now. He'll get em."

Liv hugged her grandmother. "Nana, this is Nina Vernon."

She grabbed me and hugged me. "You can call me Nana too. You are Olivia's best friend and that means you're family."

I laughed. "Thanks, Nana."

She leaned in and whispered to me. "I hear you got man-troubles. We've all had 'em, honey. You'll be safe from that jerk here! Even if he can find the place, I have a shotgun with his name on it."

She had me at the word "shotgun". I felt somewhat safe. I knew they couldn't truly protect me from a vampire, but I certainly felt safer than being at an apartment alone.

She cooked us a late lunch, and it was marvelous. I was already feeling like a healing process had begun just by being there. Food has a way of helping with that process at times. This was one of those times.

We volunteered to help with some chores around the house. Nana had severe arthritis and I didn't mind helping out. She was giving me a place to stay with no questions asked, she was feeding me, and feeding me well I might add. The company and activity was keeping my mind off my problems.

That night for dinner, Nana made chicken tetrazzini, mashed potatoes, baked asparagus, and homemade rolls. For dessert, her famous banana cream pie. It was all sinfully good, but the pie was the best damn dessert I'd ever put in my mouth. I couldn't breathe from being stuffed.

It had been a long day and night so we retired to our room. Liv tried to talk to me, but I told her I couldn't keep my eyes open. We ended up in the grandkids' room. We had bunk beds. I'd never slept in a bunk bed, but I was always up for new experiences.

As I drifted off to sleep, I fought the temptation to call Ilona. It had to be a misunderstanding. She loved me. I could straighten it all out with a phone call. Had I reacted irrationally? I felt silly. I fell asleep quickly.

Around 2 a.m., she called me. I closed myself in the bathroom to answer the call. I didn't want Liv to chastise me for answering the call.

I whispered. "Hello?"

"Darling, I know I agreed to give you time, but I've grown tired of this game. Tell me where you are and I will come to you so we can talk." The sweetness in her voice was strained and I could tell she was trying her best not to show her annoyance. Did she truly care or was it just bothering her that one of her pets ran away from home?

"I'm still thinking, Ilona. I know you've sent some of your people to look for me. I'm not coming back until you call that off."

"I'll call it off immediately if you assure me you will come and talk to me tomorrow night."

"I can't do that."

"And why not?" she demanded.

"I still need time. I think seeing you will only complicate things. I need to clear my head. I promise we will talk at some point, but it won't be tomorrow night. Take care, Ilona." I hung up, though I knew this would further anger her.

I didn't want to stay up arguing with her and letting her bully me into coming back. I also started to worry she might be able to somehow trace the cell phone signal if I stayed on any longer.

I had a hard time getting back to sleep because I was paranoid she might somehow find me and show up. Eventually I did drift off to sleep again.

I dreamed of baby sheep being slaughtered, which was quite unnerving.

I woke up to the tantalizing smells of a home cooked breakfast and thought about how much weight I was going to gain staying there. If I stayed more than a few days, Ilona might not even want me anymore! At first, I giggled to myself at the thought, but I also considered that she might still want to "dispose" of me if that is, in fact, what she did with her exes.

After we cleaned up the breakfast dishes, Liv called her boss and hashed out the details of her mysterious trip. She assured him it was a very important personal matter that could not be helped.

Then, she and I took a walk around the pond and the outer edges of the property for some exercise and something to do. The place was very homey and reminded me of my childhood in the south except that it was bitterly cold. I considered calling my grandmother, but yet again, what would I even say? I didn't want her to worry or to put her in danger.

Liv and I barely talked on our short walk. She did bring up the fact that Christmas was approaching fast. I had been so wrapped up in my own drama, I hadn't even thought about it. I was normally a giddy child about Christmas, but life had gotten in the way this year.

I think Liv was quiet because she was missing Reed, but didn't want to make me feel bad by mentioning that it was my fault we were stuck in the middle of nowhere. I kept anxiously checking my phone to see if we would hear from anyone, but it was daytime and most of the people involved were probably sleeping.

That afternoon, I was terribly bored and knew I had to think of something to do. I ended up watching television while I overheard an argument between Nana and Herb and politely pretended not to hear. They were in the kitchen discussing our visit. He apparently wasn't happy with us staying there for an undetermined amount of time, but she told him to shove it. I felt guilty, but at the same time their banter was mildly amusing.

Liv holed-up in our room and talked on the phone to Reed most of the evening. We had only been there a little over 24 hours, but I was already feeling a bit of cabin fever. I wanted out.

After another epic dinner, I felt like taking a stroll around the farm. As the skies darkened, I grew fearful and headed back inside. Liv and I retired to our room, but lay awake in the dark talking in hushed tones. I confessed to her about the phone conversation with Ilona. She wasn't happy.

"You shouldn't have answered. You didn't give her any clue as to where you were or who you were with, did you?"

"No, I'm not that stupid. She didn't give any indication that she knew I was even out of town."

"Good! Please don't answer any more calls from her while you are here. I hate to sound selfish, but I don't want my grandparents to be in harm's way."

"That's not selfish. I completely understand. I fear for myself and your family too."

She nodded. "Well, Reed said he doesn't know a lot of detail but they still seem to be looking around the area for you. She's frustrated. She had her men even rough up some of the people at your ex's club to try to get information from them."

My thoughts immediately turned to Kal. I hoped he was safe from the wrath of my crazy vampire girlfriend. "I'm pretty sure no one there would know where I was. Raphe wasn't exactly successful at having me stalked."

She sighed. "I remember having so much fun here as a child, but I'm so bored. Now I only come here for holidays and don't stay for very long."

"Yeah, I've been bored too."

"Well, how about we go to town after lunch tomorrow and goof off...see what it has to offer. I'm sure it's not much, but at least we'd be getting out of the house."

"Sounds like a hell of a plan." With that, we both slept peacefully.

***

Our adventure into town wasn't exciting. We found a little discount store and I bought a few books. There was nothing I was terribly interested in, but I craved some form of entertainment.

People stared at us everywhere we went. I hoped we weren't attracting too much attention. I started to get paranoid about it. I was looking over my shoulder.

We walked the whole length of the downtown area in 45 minutes, but we stopped in at a little diner for coffee. It reminded me vaguely of the 50's diner. We just chatted about a variety of concerns we were having. Mostly we discussed how long we could stay there. We agreed we couldn't impose on Nana and Herb much longer, but we were both scared to return to our normal lives.

I was depressed at the thought that I'd accidentally gotten her involved and it could potentially put her and her family in danger. It was done, though. I couldn't dwell on the what-ifs.

While we were sitting there, I got a call from a strange number that I didn't recognize. I didn't answer, but it started the paranoid thoughts anew. I was worried she knew where I was or that if I answered she might be able to track me down.

When we arrived back at the farmhouse, Nana informed us that a man had called. She didn't have any other info. She was concerned that it might be my ex and so she didn't stay on the phone long.

"I told him," she said, wagging her finger at an imaginary man, "I told him in no uncertain terms that there was nobody here by that name. He said to tell you," she turned around to look at the countertop. "Yeah, here it is. I wrote it down. He said if you came by I was to let you know that you had friends looking out for you." She tossed the mini spiral notebook back on the counter. "I told him I had no idea what he was talking about and flat hung up on him, but I made sure to write it down in case he meant it about being a friend."

Could it have been Kal letting me know he was okay? Was it someone from the club? Was it Raphe? I wasn't sure, but I was even more confused. Maybe it was a trick by Ilona herself. I had no way of knowing, but I chewed my fingernails all night from overanalyzing the message.

I went for a walk again after dinner. I walked around the edge of the woods and then on to the pond. It started to get dark, but I could just see the beginnings of starlight reflecting off the half-frozen water. It was so still and peaceful.

My mind was clear and empty except for the beauty that I was embracing. I finally turned to walk back towards the house when I heard a twig snap behind me. I stopped breathing for a moment. I couldn't decide whether to run or call for help. I turned quickly to find a man standing there and I almost fainted. My eyes focused on the face as it grew closer. It was Graham.

"Hello, lovely."

"Graham! I've never been so happy to see someone." I hugged him tightly. "Please tell me you aren't here on business for Ilona? I'm not going back willingly."

"No. She sent me off to keep me from you and now she plans to harm you. I can't let that happen. I'm only sorry that I told her about you."

I raised an eyebrow. "You told her about me? What do you mean?"

"I mean I had seen you sing and I told her of your gift."

"You keep calling it a gift. I just sing."

"I tried to explain it before. Your voice reaches everyone, but vampires in particular because of how your voice affects us. It touches us, when normally very little does. While you are singing, we feel human for a brief time. I don't know how or why, but it is a magical experience." He pulled me into him and held me tightly.

"Thank you." I knew I had made a mistake in not trusting Graham completely. I should have listened to him from day one. I was blinded by my attraction to

Ilona. I'd never before felt so stupid. "How did you know what was going on?"

"I had some employees who kept me informed of what was going on between you and Ilona. As soon as I got word that you had left, I made arrangements for transport back to the U.S."

"Thank goodness. I've been so scared."

"I don't know if I can truly protect you from her. She is older than me and she has lots of minions at her disposal. I will certainly try. Right now, she doesn't know where you are. I think maybe we should get moving tomorrow night and not stay in one place for long."

"Okay. Shall we take Liv?"

"I suppose that's up to her, but I think she should get back to her life."

I nodded. "I will try and talk her into going home. I've endangered her too much already."

He gently touched my face. "Is there somewhere on the property I can hide out for the night?"

"I'll ask Liv. Let me go find her and I will bring her out. Meet me at the edge of the woods behind the house in 10 minutes?"

"I'll be there." He grinned at me. "I know that now is not the time or place...and that you can't feel the same for me right now...but I want you to know that I love you."

"I know."

I went straight to Liv in the bedroom. "Graham is here to help."

"Graham?" She looked at me, perplexed.

"I think I told you about him. He works for Ilona, but he loves me and was sent off so that she could try to seduce me."

"Oh, that guy. Are you sure we can trust him?"

"He tried to warn me about her. I think that speaks volumes." She followed me outside to greet him.

Graham stood still, waiting patiently as we approached. He held out his hand to her and she reluctantly shook it while I introduced them. She seemed to be intimidated by him, but I couldn't imagine why. I guess it was because he was a vampire, but out of all the ones I'd met, Graham was the least intimidating.

He smiled reassuringly at her. "We have to leave as soon as it gets dark tomorrow. You may come if you wish, but it is dangerous, and I'd rather you head home to lessen your involvement."

She nodded. "I'll stay the night here after you leave and head back the next morning. I hope everything goes smoothly." She turned to me. "You'll call me and let me know you're okay? I know we've only recently become friends, but I care about you. Please be careful."

"We will." I glanced at Graham. "Is there somewhere safe nearby he can stay during the day tomorrow? Obviously we don't want to have to explain who he is to your grandparents..."

She thought for a few moments. "Well, we could sneak

you into the basement later in the night after they've gone to bed. But if you hear someone heading down the basement steps, take shelter in the broom closet because it's rarely used."

"I guess that'll be the plan. We'll come fetch you here later on." I smiled at him.

He cleared his throat. "Can I have some time alone with you to talk before you go to bed?"

"Yeah. Give me a half hour or so to shower and get bed clothes on and I'll come out the back to meet you."

When we headed back into the house together, Liv wanted me to consider her doubts. "Are you sure you trust him?"

"Implicitly."

"You don't exactly have a good track record for discerning who is trustworthy, so you'll have to understand why I'm being skeptical. What if he drives you straight back to the club?"

"He won't do that. He tried to warn me how she was but I didn't listen. I wanted to believe that she was perfect."

"Alright." She hugged me. "I'm going to bed. We'll just tell them about us leaving tomorrow. I'm sure Nana will make a feast."

"Thank you for being here for me, Liv. I'm lucky to have you as a friend."

She smiled at me as she shut the bedroom door. "Have fun with your new boyfriend."

"Hey, that's not..." I bristled at the implication. I still cared for Ilona. I resented the idea that I'd jump into another relationship before the current one ended. Then again, I was attracted to Graham. I always had been.

While I was in the shower, I thought of the lovemaking with Ilona and how new and exciting it had been compared to all the other lovers in my life. I'd never even considered that I might be bi-sexual, but I had to admit that the sex at least was the best I'd ever had.

Despite this, I found myself aroused at the idea of Graham touching me. It almost felt like a betrayal of the love I shared with Ilona. I didn't know what to think of myself. I was ashamed. Had it ever been love with Ilona or was it just lust all along?

When I met him at the edge of the woods, he looked deeply into me with his kind eyes. "I really do love you. I know I've said it a few times, but I don't think you understand…"

I interrupted him. "I know you mean it. Or at least you believe it yourself. I don't think you truly know me well enough, but I enjoy the attention and I'm glad you're here for me."

"I will always be there for you as long as I live."

"You aren't exactly alive though, are you?" We both laughed awkwardly.

"Let me rephrase that. I will be there for you as long as Ilona doesn't have me killed."

"Well, that's a buzzkill." I started walking deeper into the woods. I'd been afraid to do so, but the moonlight was bright and I wasn't afraid with him there.

He followed and grabbed my arm. "Listen, I know I've made some mistakes. For instance, telling Ilona about your beauty and your gift...I wouldn't have done so if I'd known the end result. However, I'm willing to wait out the heartbreak you are going through."

I felt a tinge of anger. "Heartbreak? I haven't decided the fate of our relationship yet and I think it's a bit arrogant of you to believe that if I do leave her that I would consider you…" I trailed off.

Deep down, I knew that I couldn't go back to Ilona. I felt unsafe and that level of mistrust could never be repaired. I was just reluctant to let go.

There was that heartbroken look on his face again. He started to walk back towards the house. I turned and followed him. I couldn't stand seeing him that way. I'd done it to him too many times before.

"Please wait. I'm sorry. Of course I'm going to leave her, but it's just hard to turn off your feelings like a light switch."

He stopped about 10 feet away and looked at me with a distance in his eyes. The hurt was still there. I walked up to him slowly, without saying a word. I looped my arms around his neck and we stood like that for an eternity, face to face...our eyes delving deep into each other.

I wanted him to kiss me, but it still felt wrong for me to be doing anything so soon with someone else. I could tell he was weighing the thought himself. My breath was so close it was touching his lips. He slid a hand along my hip and pulled me closer for a hug. My head went to his shoulder instinctively and he caressed my hair. The whole interaction felt perfectly natural. He felt like home.

When we finally pulled away from each other he was crying. His eyes were bloody. "Are you okay?"

"I'm fine. Wonderful, in fact. This is what happens when a vampire cries."

I grabbed his hand and squeezed it gently. "I'm going to go get some sleep and rest up. I bet by now Nana and Herb are asleep. Come to the back door in about 5 minutes and I will help you sneak into the basement."

Sure enough, all the lights were off. I had to be really careful not to make a whole bunch of noise trying to get around the house in the dark. I had to use my cell phone to be able to see anything.

I ushered him in and into the basement door. Before he shut it behind him, he grabbed my face with both hands and just caressed my cheeks while looking into my eyes. "Soon." he said.

I stumbled back a step.

"Soon." he said again softly and then shut the door behind himself. I went to bed practically purring like a kitten.

***

When I woke up the next day, Nana had starting prepping for an our goodbye dinner already. She fed us until we thought our stomachs would explode. I was tempted to go check on Graham, but I resisted. Nightfall would come soon enough. Nana wouldn't let us help clean since it was the last day of our visit. I was going crazy having to wait.

When we weren't eating, I spent some time in my bottom bunk. I read a self-help book that I'd picked up from the discount store. It wasn't my normal choice of genre. There was lots of advice about finding your self-worth before seeking out relationships. I decided to be resolute in staying single for a while. If Graham really did love me, he'd wait, right?

I packed my luggage and put it on the porch. I realized we hadn't quite discussed our mode of transportation since Liv was going home. I snuck into the basement while Nana and Herb were watching TV. I opened the broom closet and he looked like he was ready to pounce on me. He thought was caught. "Oh, it's you. Are you ready to go?"

"Almost. I still have to say goodbye to everyone. Do we have a ride?"

"Yes, the ride I came in is hidden in a field about a half mile from here. I will go retrieve it for us if you help me sneak out."

"Liv's grandparents are downstairs. I don't know how I can sneak you by them."

"Show me to a window."

I led him to the bedroom window and opened it. "It's a long drop. Are you sure you can get down safely?"

"I think you'll find I'm quite agile. I'll meet you at the end of the driveway in a few minutes?"

"Yes." Before I could say anything else, he'd grabbed onto the trellis and leaped the rest of the way to the ground. I had a brief heart palpitation, but I calmed down when I saw that he was unharmed.

We had a heartfelt goodbye with Nana. She made Liv promise to come back for the holidays. They were coming up fast. Even Herb seemed sad to see me go. Maybe he liked me better now that I was leaving. I wasn't sure.

Liv followed me down the driveway. "I told them a friend was coming to get you and that things were going to be okay. I don't want them to worry. They've grown attached to you."

"Thank you. I care for them too. And I'll miss Nana's pie most of all."

She laughed. "Yes, I always miss the pies when I'm away myself."

We embraced. "Let me know what Reed hears and we'll keep in touch while on the road."

"Okay. Be safe. I'll be worried sick."

We got in the car. She shut the door for me and waved as we drove away.

Goodbye, sweet friend. I hoped I'd see her again.

10 ON THE ROAD AGAIN

He drove like a little old lady. You'd expect a vampire to have a devil-may-care attitude, but not Graham, apparently. I wasn't sure if he was always this way or if he was doing it to be overprotective of me.

We didn't talk much on the ride, but he would occasionally glance over at me and smile. He seemed to be enjoying looking at me as much as I was enjoying his attention.

I knew that we were heading west, but we'd never spoken about where we were going. Curiosity got the best of me a few hours in and I finally asked. "Where are we going?"

"I figured we could just stop in random towns so we will be harder to track. I would like to end up in Las Vegas because that's where the largest vampire population in North America is and we're less likely to be noticed."

"Wow. Vegas? I would think somewhere like New York or L.A. would be more obvious vampire havens since they are bigger in general."

"Think about it. There's stuff going on 24 hours a day in Vegas. Lots of things for a vampire to get into."

"Hmm. I guess that makes sense." I'd never been to Vegas so I was more than a little excited. I'd never traveled much.

We stopped in Utica, New York to rest at a swanky hotel. He paid for it, despite my protests. He got us a room with double beds and I found I was a little disappointed by that.

When I tried to sleep, I kept thinking paranoid thoughts about people following us and I'd wondered what Graham was thinking and if he was sleeping. I lay awake for what seemed like an eternity before I spoke up. "Graham?"

"Yes, lovely."

"Are you awake?"

"Yes."

"I'm having trouble sleeping. Do you mind if I get into bed with you?"

I could almost hear the smile in his voice when he responded. "Of course, if you wish."

I slipped into bed and draped my arm across his chest. He rubbed my arm with his hand. I was feeling safe in seconds. "Thank you again."

"It's nothing. When you dedicate yourself to someone, you will do anything for them."

"You've dedicated yourself to me?"

"I have been dedicated to you for...a long time." It was a little creepy the way he said it.

"How long?"

"A long time."

I glared at him. "How long?!"

Just then, my phone rang and we both almost jumped out of our skin. I didn't recognize the number, but it was similar to the one in Ilona's office so I assumed it was another line at the club. I looked towards Graham in the darkness as if he'd know what to do. I just waited for it to stop ringing before I could breathe again. I was terrified.

I held onto Graham even tighter, with my body tensed-up against him. He kissed me on the forehead and I eventually relaxed and drifted off to sleep.

***

When I woke up the next day around lunch, I was torn. Should I stay by his side until dark? I ultimately decided to go with my gut instinct and by gut instinct, I mean I was starving.

I left a note for him and walked to a nearby restaurant for something to eat. After that, I went for a walk and called Liv. She was on her way home. I was hoping she'd heard from Reed. I wanted to know any news regarding Ilona and her search for me. Alas, she hadn't heard a word. She was sad to go back to work after having a few lazy days. I thanked her again for being there for me.

I went back to the hotel room and curled up with Graham for a nap. I was feeling fatigued a lot lately because I was emotionally drained. When I woke up, it was dark. Graham was just a few inches from my face and he was watching me sleep.

I cleared my throat. "Can I help you?"

"Yes, you can fall in love with me."

I turned away in the bed and faced the window. "That's not something I can force. I still love Ilona. I don't know if I will ever be able to feel that way about you." Even as I said it, I knew it wasn't true. I already felt something, but I wasn't quite sure what it was.

He rubbed my shoulder gently. "Please don't be upset. I understand. I hope that you understand that I love you anyway and that I will wait patiently for the chance that you may love me."

My heart swelled at his words. His presence was a comfort to me.

We were soon on the road again. I had him stop at a gas station for snacks, but he put the pedal down to put some more distance between us and Underland.

On the ride, I nervously told him about everything that had gone on since he was sent away, including the fact that Raphe was also looking for me. I tried to skip over details of my relationship with Ilona, but he dragged them out of me.

I apologized for not listening to him. "I realize now that she's dangerous. I don't know if she has killed her past lovers, but I certainly think she's capable of harming me. I'm scared."

He put his hand on mine. "I will not let her harm you."

Again my phone rang in the middle of the night. It was the same phone number as the previous night. I stared at it while it rang. I wished for her to give up on me and let it go, but she was not that type of person. I knew that she was probably realizing it was over. That could be a very dangerous thing.

We stopped again. I think it was Iowa. I wasn't even sure. By the time we stopped, I was delirious. This time, we were stuck in a single bed. I wasn't complaining because I felt safe that way. I curled up next to his still body and drifted off just as day broke.

I guess I was just exhausted. I didn't wake up again until it was dark outside. He was propped up on his pillow just looking at me. "You've got to stop doing that. It's creepy."

"I'm just taking in every moment that I'm close to you. I'm going to memorize you just in case we are never this close again. I leaned over into his chest while he was laying sideways. I tried to hug him. He shifted his position a little until we were face to face. I closed my eyes and enjoyed the warmth of his gaze. The urge hit and I grabbed his face and kissed him hard. He held me back and slowed me down. He wrapped his tongue gently around mine. It was like he knew the perfect way to maneuver my mouth.

I let a little moan slip out. I was very aroused. I'd been in denial, but the sexual tension with him had been there all along and the trip made it worse. He slid his hand down the small of my back and pressed my body against his so that I could feel how ready he was for me.

I came close to losing control, but I came to my senses and tried to push him away. He was lost in the moment and I was not strong enough to actually push him. He finally released me after a few intense moments. It was enough to remind me of how different it was to be with a vampire. It made me feel weak and helpless. I immediately got up and got ready to leave.

***

The rest of the trip we didn't talk about what happened and we didn't sleep in the same bed. We only talked about necessities. He was constantly asking if I needed food or anything else since he didn't need the same things that I did. I was lost in thoughts about how much I still cared for Ilona and my burgeoning attraction to Graham.

When we finally pulled into Vegas, the tension and worries melted away as I turned into a giddy child upon seeing all the lights. "Ooh! Look at that!" I exclaimed at least a dozen times.

We had a few hours until daylight so we went to a few casinos in the older part of town. This was the area you usually saw in movies about Vegas, but there honestly wasn't much going on there anymore.

He treated me to a buffet since I'd only eaten a few actual meals on the trip. He watched me pigging-out with an amused look on his face.

I was curious about vampire clubs, but he said that we didn't want to draw unnecessary attention to ourselves. Instead he took me to a strip club and we had some drinks and laughs while letting some girls dance for us privately. One girl was a particular favorite of both of us. She was a tiny-framed blond who didn't seem to understand how to properly use her own sexuality. She was horrible at dancing, but we enjoyed talking to her.

We crashed in our hotel room. In my bed, I felt the stirrings of arousal. I ached for him. I wasn't sure if it was the drinks or the close quarters of our trip. I contemplated sneaking into his bed, but I couldn't get past my fear of another failed vampire relationship. So instead I lay there and replayed the kiss over and over in my head until I fell asleep.

My phone rang about 4 pm. I didn't recognize the number but since it was daytime, I assumed it was not Ilona. I walked out of the hotel room and down the hallway to the lobby to answer the phone.

"Hello?"

"It's good to hear your voice, Nina. I've been worried about you."

"Kal! What's up? Why are you worried?"

"I've been watching Underland and hadn't seen you in about a week. I was kinda worried the vampires had killed you."

"I'm fine. I'm hiding out from the vampires and Raphe. Is he still looking for me?"

"Of course. He's real angry that he can't get at you. He knows about the vampires now. Someone told him. At first he didn't believe it, but after he sent a few thugs to spy and feel out the place, he started to believe."

I groaned. "I sure know how to pick 'em."

He laughed and I grimaced. I explained what was going on. "The owner of the club is looking for me too. We kind of broke up and she isn't happy about it." I was suddenly mindful of just how crazy it all sounded. Was I really worth the trouble of everyone involved?

I assured him I'd be okay and asked him to keep me informed of any changes going on back home. He agreed.

When we hung up, I called Liv to let her know we had settled in. I didn't tell her where we were in fear that someone might drill her for information. She gave us what little details she had from Reed. Apparently, no one had seen Ilona at the club for the past few days. Supposedly, she still had people searching for me, but had no clue where I was. It made me nervous that she wasn't there. Not even her inner-circle knew where she had gone.

"When I got back to the room, it was only minutes before Graham woke up. I told him what I had found out. "Hey, why hasn't she tried to call you? Aren't you her right-hand man? Isn't that going to seem suspicious if you aren't in touch?"

"I threw out my phone when I arrived back in the

states. I was afraid she would trace it. I'm sure by now she knows I'm involved. She has probably contacted her people in Europe and realizes I'm not with Zaleska. She knows how I feel about you. This will not be a surprise to her."

"Oh." I was even more afraid. Not only had I run away, but I'd run away with her best employee who was in love with me. She was likely furious. The idea of Ilona furious was terrifying.

"We had a huge falling-out when she sent me away. I knew it was only a matter of time before I found an excuse to walk away from my position."

"I'm sorry, I feel like I'm the cause of all this."

"You are not the cause of all this. Ilona is accustomed to getting her way at all costs. She married young and was turned into a vampire while young and it made her incredibly mean. I know her very well. She is my creator."

This was news to me. "She what?"

"She is my creator. I will always feel love for her because of it, but I also understand the good things and bad things about her like no other. We were even lovers briefly, but like I've already explained, vampires don't stay lovers long."

"I had no idea. How did neither of you feel that this knowledge should be shared with me?" I felt anger rising in me.

"I guess we didn't feel it was important. There was no conspiracy to keep it from you."

I wasn't sure why it bothered me that they had slept together, but it did. I'm not even sure which one of them I was more jealous about. They had a history together that I was left out of. I was again frustrated that I didn't know anything about them.

There was a level of mystery about vampires that was hard to deal with. They had so much past that you could never really know everything and it was frustrating. I always had a million questions floating around to ask, but never seemed to find the right time for asking.

"Graham, I'm afraid. Her being missing from the club...frankly, it scares me."

"That could be for any number of reasons. She has lots of business obligations. It could be that it's something completely unrelated. But it could be that she is following a lead about us. There's no point in worrying about it."

He got out of his bed and slid an arm around me. I was wearing a t-shirt and pajama pants. I was feeling very unsexy. I backed away from him.

"No, you're not running from me again." He forcibly kissed me. I only fought it for seconds. It was like fireworks went off inside my body. He was kissing my neck and nibbling my earlobes. I slowly moved us towards the bed. I wasn't even thinking about sex at that point. I was just wanting more of his touch.

He slid my pajama pants off and started kissing my inner thighs. Any protest I had died before it could leave my mouth. He kissed his way down my stomach and slid off my panties.

I was paralyzed. I couldn't move or breathe. I just knew I wanted this. After a few minutes of licking me into utopia, he stopped abruptly. I thought I might start begging for more.

He kissed his way up my stomach and stopped when he got to my face. He looked into my eyes. "Do you want me?"

"Yes. I do."

He looked at me hesitantly. He was waiting for me to change my mind, but I practically begged him with my eyes.

He took off the rest of my clothes and his own with a feverish quickness. I found myself a little intimidated by his size, but there was no stopping what was happening. He slid into me slowly and I let out an involuntary moan.

I was so wet that his size didn't matter. My body shuddered with every slow, steady thrust. His movements were deliberate and precise. He had love-making down to a science. He alternated from lightly pinching my nipples to grabbing my hips while he thrusted deep inside of me. He kissed me with a hunger. He made very little sound, but he did occasionally let out a whimper.

I didn't want it to stop, but eventually my body betrayed me. When I orgasmed, it came in waves and he kept on thrusting. He finally threw back his head and closed his eyes before slowing to a halt.

I woke up at 2 am and he was staring at me as usual. He was caressing my body. I drifted off again, but when morning came we made love again. We didn't leave the room that night or day. It was a magnificent blur.

***

When I finally got up, I ordered some room service and watched him sleep. From what I knew so far, he was a beautiful creature, inside and out. Unlike Ilona, he never seemed intimidating or scary. I knew it was too soon to say it, but I did love him. I knew it.

When he woke, we showered together and got dressed up to go out. He caressed me, but made no attempt to seduce me again. I was more than a little relieved. I was exhausted and somewhat sore from our intense love-making sessions.

We went to a club and sat around enjoying the drinks and each other's company. We discussed only light-hearted topics and stared at each other, lovingly.

At some point, I went to the bathroom and when I came back there was a man sitting with Graham. I approached slowly and cautiously. Graham glanced at me from over his shoulder. I could tell from the look on his face that this was bad. I started to turn and head back to the bathroom, but the man caught my eye. "Oh, this must be your lady friend! Don't be shy, darling. Come and sit."

"Darling, this is Crin. He's an old friend. I haven't seen him in ages. Crin, this is my inamorata, Jill."

"Hello, Jill. You're quite a catch. I wish Graham hadn't already laid claim to you..."

I looked at Graham and he looked slightly amused. "I...Thanks. I'm quite dedicated to Graham."

"Good. Good. So where are you from?" He looked at me expectantly. I wasn't sure how much I should tell this man. I looked at Graham again.

Graham cleared his throat. "She's from Mississippi, originally. I picked her up and decided we needed to take a little vacation to get to know each other better." He smiled at me.

"She can't speak for herself?"

"She knows her place. She is mine and therefore, she does not want to anger me by showing too much attention to you."

I almost choked on the drink I was sipping. It was strange hearing this come out of Graham's mouth.

Crin laughed. "I'm jealous. Beautiful and submissive. Mmm." The guy was creeping me out. They chatted a little bit more, but Graham was quick to ask for the check. "

We've got to get back to our room, Crin. Still need to get to know her more." He winked at Crin.

Crin nodded, knowingly. "Maybe I'll see you around. I'll be here for another couple of days. Tell Ilona I said hello."

We went straight back to the room and I could tell he was bothered.

"We have to leave again. Crin is another vampire created by Ilona. He hasn't worked for her in many years, but we still run the risk that he may mention he has seen us to someone. It may get back to her."

"That's a lot of what-ifs. I think you should calm down."

"We can't risk it. Let's pack up and leave now. Maybe we should head into Canada. There's not much vampire population there…"

I plopped down on the edge of the bed. "NO. I don't want to travel anymore. I'm sick of it. It was exhausting and I'm not ready to endure that again. Besides, I'm having fun here with you and there's no guarantee that he will tell her anything."

"You do have a point." He looked exasperated.

"I think maybe we should let things calm down for a few more days and then head home. We can just face this thing head-on. I don't want to spend the rest of my life on the run." I hoped he'd listen to reason.

"Are you insane?" He looked at me incredulously.

"It makes sense. As long as I'm running, they will be hunting me. If I just go home and turn myself over to them and just try to rationalize the situation, then we might have a fighting chance."

"I don't know much about your ex, but I know that Ilona will not just let things go. Let's think about this a little bit longer, maybe discuss it more."

"Okay, but we can't run forever. Please think about the effect this is having on me. Being afraid all the time is draining." I gave him my best pouty face to lighten things up and try to win him over to my side.

"I know." He sat with me on the bed and kissed me on the forehead. I slipped my arms around him and he forgot about the discussion at least temporarily.

We snuggled up together and I fell asleep. The travel and weird sleeping schedule made me feel like I was sleeping too much, but I wasn't sure what to do about it.

The next night, we headed to the strip club again but our favorite blond wasn't there. We still had fun getting private dances from various girls. Mostly, Graham just seemed to enjoy watching me get lavished with attention from the ladies. He paid them extra for being good to me.

After that, we went to a dance club called Luxure. We danced. He was a horrible dancer, but it didn't stop us from having a good time. I made sure to rub my body against his whenever possible. I started to enjoy the art of driving him crazy. I loved knowing exactly how much he wanted me.

When we went back to the room, he closed the door behind him and gave me a look like he could rip off my clothes. I changed into my nightgown and lay down like I was going to sleep. He stripped and curled up behind me. I could feel exactly how aroused he was, but I decided to toy with him. He kissed the back of my neck. "Oh, um...I don't know if I'm in the mood tonight, Graham. I am a little tired from all the dancing." I yawned.

He rolled over onto his back and audibly sighed. "Okay. Rest up." I could hear the disappointment and frustration in his voice.

I grinned, but I was facing away and he didn't catch that. I slyly slid off my panties and threw them on the floor on my side of the bed. I threw a leg over him and straddled his lean torso. He was caught off-guard and moaned a little. He groped and grabbed at me roughly.

Eventually, he couldn't stand not being in control so he switched positions and moved me off of him and mounted me. From there, it was a frenzied tornado of lust. My mind was blown. It felt wonderful to feel so wanted. With him, there were no doubts of exactly how he felt.

I was awake for hours after we finished. I just let the lingering waves of good feeling from making love with him keep washing over me. In the dark, I wondered how I'd lived my life without him before now. I assumed he was resting when I leaned over and kissed him on the cheek. "I love you," I whispered.

I turned over to sleep and a few moments later, he spooned me and ran his hand over my naked stomach. "And I love you, my lovely songstress."

My heart raced and surely my face had reddened but it was dark and no one saw. I guess I wasn't ready for that confession to be public, but there it was. It was the truth. I fell asleep with his arm around my waist and his naked body pressed against mine.

***

When I opened my eyes again, he was gone. I had a

moment of panic. I looked outside the door and window. I was afraid to go anywhere because I knew he didn't have a phone and the idea of us getting separated was frightening.

I sat down on the bed and tried to calmly assess the situation, but in reality I was a mess. Hopefully he'd be right back. If someone had come to get him, surely I'd have been woken up or also taken...right? Every minute that passed, I think my heart rate went up.

I was just considering calling the front desk to ask if they'd seen him when he came waltzing through the door. "Where the hell have you been?"

"I ran out to get you some Chinese food. I remembered you'd mentioned a craving for it when we were out dancing last night."

I hugged him tightly. "You scared the shit out of me! I thought of one of Ilona's thugs had come for you while I was sleeping or something! Why didn't you tell me or at least leave a note?"

"I'm sorry to scare you, dear. You looked so peaceful and beautiful sleeping and I didn't want to wake you."

I fell into his arms as sobs wracked my body. "I can't stand this fear."

"I know." He stared at the floor as he held me. "We'll go home whenever you are ready."

"Can we leave tomorrow night?"

"If that is what you wish." He wiped the tears from my cheeks.

"Sort of. I am dreading the car ride home." I grinned at him and the tears began to dry.

"I can make flight arrangements."

"What about the car?"

He let out a good hearty laugh. "It's a loaner from Ilona. I'm not really concerned about it at the moment."

I rubbed the tears from my eyes and laughed too. "Oh darn. Will she ever forgive us?"

"Maybe. I'll make the proper calls for travel

arrangements while you eat your food. It's getting cold."

"Thank you for the Chinese food. It was thoughtful of you."

I ate some of it. I didn't have the heart to tell him that Chinese food sounded disgusting since I'd just woken up.

After he finished with his phone calls, he sat next to me on the bed. "What do you want to do? It's our last night in Vegas and the town is ours."

"Stay in." I kissed him, slowly but deeply. I'll leave out the colorful details, but it was magical. The sex with Graham just seemed to get better and better.

11 DANSE MACABRE

When we were done, we just caressed one another and talked about random thoughts that came up. After a while, I proposed that we should actually do something on our last night in Vegas. "I want to go to a vampire club. I've only ever been to Underland."

"Are you sure? We're still on the run...it's not safe."

"Well by the time she gets word, we'll be on our way there anyway, right?"

He sighed. "I guess so." I could tell he wasn't so sure about my idea.

"Well, you pick the place."

"The nicest one is 'Danse Macabre' and it's been around for ages."

"Sounds wonderful." I showered and donned my little black dress. I put on my darkest red lipstick. I pinned back some of my unruly curls with a little red flower barrette. I wanted to be beautiful on our last night out.

While was getting ready, Graham went out and bought himself a new pinstripe suit. This one was a black suit with more distinct white lines. He looked quite dapper and had his hair spiked up in different directions as usual. He had on his glasses, which he most likely didn't need but wore most of the time anyway. He was a classy and intelligent sort of sexy and even though it wasn't my usual type, I found him irresistible.

When we spotted one another, we both just paused for a moment and took in the sight. I was primping in the bathroom mirror and he just stood in the doorway and watched me. When we walked out of the hotel, I couldn't be more proud that I was on his arm.

Things got even more interesting when he opened

the door to a limousine and informed me we'd be riding in it. I had some champagne on the ride to the club. I didn't really care for the stuff, but decided to have some since it was provided for us.

There was a line to get in at the club, but Graham worked his way to the front and spoke a few words in a whisper to the bouncer and he waved us in. I had never felt so important in my life!

A hostess led us to a private balcony booth overlooking the dance floor. Everyone there was beautiful. I had never seen so many attractive people in one place. "Are these all vampires?" I asked Graham.

"No, but they are very selective about what humans to let in unless they are with a vampire of significance."

"Are you a vampire of significance, then?"

"Not really, but I work for Ilona and she is one of the most feared and respected vampires in America."

"Is that what you told the bouncer?"

"I told him I was here on business for Ilona."

"Oh." I relaxed for a bit and then snuggled up next to him in the circular booth.

For a while, we just enjoyed the view of the dance floor and each other. I wanted to dance, but he told me to go ahead and he'd enjoy watching me. He said he'd join me soon.

I went down and made my way through the dance floor to seek out a partner. It didn't take long before a group of beautiful women accepted me into their fold. They looked like they were teenagers, but they could have been vampires so I wasn't sure about their true age.

We were writhing around to the beats together in a circle. It was almost ritualistic. It felt so right. We laughed at certain moments when we noticed each other. We mimicked each other's movements perfectly. I'd glance up occasionally to see Graham studying us. He'd grin at me from time to time.

I was starting to grow tired so I considered heading back up to sit with him. I turned and saw a man entering the circle of girls. It was Crin. "Hello again, Jill. So wonderful to see you without your lover." He grabbed my wrist and pulled me off the dance floor. It happened so fast that I didn't have a chance to fight him off. I glanced up at the booth and Graham wasn't there. My only hope was that he had spotted Crin before I did and was already headed to my rescue.

Crin pulled me down a hallway filled with the glow of fluorescent lights and out the exit door. From what I could tell, we were behind the club and there was no one around. I tried to pull away from him back towards the door, but it felt like my arm might pop right out of the socket if I yanked any harder. I tried to scream and he pulled me by my hair and close to his face. "Scream again and I smash your face into this stone wall."

I wanted to cry, but I kept on my brave face. "What do you want?" I was afraid he'd found out who I was and wanted to earn bounty by either returning me to Ilona or killing me for her and I didn't like the thought of either one.

"I want you, honeybuns. You are too cute for nice-guy. I think you need some spice in your life."

I breathed a sigh of relief. I decided to play along and hope that I could buy some time for Graham to find me. "Oh...maybe so. Tell me what's so spicy about you."

I flashed him my best grin and he lessened his grip on me. "I'm a bad boy and that makes me much more fun."

"Mmm. I do like having fun. And I love vampires. They make much better lovers than boring old humans." I leaned in closer to him.

He let go of me and grabbed my chin roughly. He forced his lips on mine and shoved his tongue in my mouth. I felt queasy, but I didn't push him away. I let him finish kissing me and then when he pulled away, I turned to run. He grabbed my hair before I got 3 feet away. I screamed at the pain in my scalp. "Tsk tsk, little one. You shouldn't have tried to fool me. That just makes me angry. I may have my fun with you and then drain you dry."

He grabbed my wrist again and started pulling me around toward the side of the building. Just then, Graham burst through the back door screaming, "Nina?" He spotted us and rushed over. "Let her go." His voice boomed in our direction.

He let go of my wrist and I had to fight back tears. My wrists and scalp were burning from the assault. Adrenaline was coursing through my veins, amplifying the pain and terror.

Crin ran at Graham. I retreated back to the exit door, just waiting to see what happened, but ready to flee back to the relative safety of the club at a moment's notice if necessary.

For a bit, no one landed a hit on the other. It was a power struggle, but Crin finally got the best of Graham and slammed his head into the wall. I recoiled in horror. Crin looked at me and this gave Graham an opportunity. He grabbed Crin, wrestled him to the ground, and got on top of him. He started pounding on him.

I was horrified at what I was seeing, but I was speechless. Part of me wanted him to stop, but I was scared that Crin would only hurt him worse if he got the chance to get up.

Finally, I spoke up. "Graham, please don't kill him." When he looked at me, I was startled by the viciousness I saw in his eyes.

The look of horror on my face must have brought back the Graham I knew and loved. He stopped and got up. He dragged his foe around the side of the building toward the front door. I followed cautiously. He dumped the limp Crin in front of the bouncer. A few girls in the crowd screamed at the sight. "This vampire tried to attack my inamorata and he has paid the price."

The bouncer looked at Graham incredulously. "What do you want me to do with him?"

Graham gave a nonchalant smile. "I don't care."

I followed Graham back into the club while we waited for our limo to pick us up. I tried to calm my fear, but I was horrified by what had happened. He seemed distant, but he held me close.

We hurried back to the hotel when the limo came. He made me pack my things before we went to bed in case anything happened while we tried to sleep. I hoped we could make it onto the plane without incident. I wanted out of Vegas as soon as possible, but it was nearing dawn and we were stuck.

I curled up in his arms and it was hours before I

finally fell asleep. I couldn't stop thinking about the viciousness in his eyes when he was beating Crin to a pulp. I was afraid of how I was in so much shit since I entered this world of vampires. On one hand, I still loved Graham and knew that he was nothing like Ilona, but on the other hand I also wished I had never found out about vampires.

I think I'd have been better off staying at my crummy convenience store job and being completely naive about the damned blood-suckers.

He checked the hotel hallway and lobby before we left the room. We left the car at the airport and boarded the plane. I didn't get enough sleep. I was exhausted, but I couldn't sleep for the whole trip. We didn't speak at all during the flight. I wasn't sure where his head was, but mine was being pulled in a dozen different directions.

When we arrived, it was so late (or early, depending on how you look at it) that we rented a car and checked into the hotel nearest the airport. I passed out as soon as my head hit the pillow.

That evening, I woke up before Graham. I watched him resting. His face had transformed back to the wonderful, loving creature I had fallen in love with. I pushed aside my fear and confusion from the fight. I laid my head on his chest and waited for him to wake.

When he finally came out of his deep vampire sleep, he rubbed my shoulders gently. I kissed him and I could tell that he was getting heated up, but I pulled away from him.

"What's wrong, lovely?"

"I'm too preoccupied with what's going to happen. I'm not really in the mood right now."

"I understand. Whatever you wish, darling."

"I'm sorry..." I wasn't sure what else to say.

He kissed me on the forehead. "Do not fret. We have plenty of time for that."

I didn't express my concern that maybe we wouldn't. It all depended on our survival at the showdown between my exes. Wow, it seemed silly to think of it that way, but there it was.

We had a little bit of a drive from the airport to

town. I called Liv during the car ride. I informed her we were coming back to town to face things. She wished us luck, but wanted nothing to do with the big mess. I certainly couldn't blame her.

My nerves were shot. I was jumpy and anxious. I was terrified, but also ready to get it over with. I tried to rehearse what I would say to Ilona in my head, but I couldn't gauge exactly how it would go over. There was nothing to truly prepare you for going head-to-head with an angry ex-girlfriend.

I decided to go to her first to get that out of the way. I would worry about Raphe later. He was small potatoes compared to Ilona. I hadn't even considered what I'd say to him.

12 ALL MY EXES

We pulled up in front of Underland, and Graham grasped my hand and squeezed it. I wished suddenly that it was more than just the two of us, that we had reinforcements. It probably wouldn't have mattered. With all the pawns that Ilona had at her disposal, if she decided to kill us both there was nothing either of us could do to stop her.

When we stepped out of our car in front of the club, the bouncer was on the phone in seconds. I assumed he was alerting Ilona. Everyone glared at us when we walked inside. It seemed that virtually the whole crowd knew what was going on.

We started down that long hallway and it felt like my guts were trembling. We paused for a second in front of her door. The hall guards were looking at us like they thought we'd gone insane. Graham raised his hand to knock and her stern voice spoke up. "Come in."

We walked in cautiously and I sat down, but Graham remained standing. I figured I might as well be sitting if I was going to die anyway. Besides that, I wasn't sure if I had the strength to stand at the moment.

I focused on keeping my breath steady. Everything went down so fast, I thought back to my first encounter with Graham and his quip about breathing being essential. I probably would have chuckled at the thought if I'd had the intestinal fortitude.

"Well, you have returned. Do you wish to apologize?" She glared directly at me and seemed to ignore Graham's presence.

"Apologize?" I bit my lip at this incredulous thought, then continued. "You frightened me and threatened me, despite claiming to love me! All I did was take some time to think, which is a normal thing when you are having second thoughts about the validity of your relationship."

She rammed her fist into the desk, sending vibrations through the whole room. "I have never shown you anything but love, you ungrateful brat! I have given you everything your heart desires. It is you who turned a blind eye to my true nature, you who ignored your own instincts to love me. You made your own mistakes and must now deal with the consequences."

By now, the fear was being overtaken by fury bubbling to the surface. "It was a mistake," I shouted. "Love is blind. I loved you and chose to only see the positive in you. Sadly, I still do see positive in you." I could see the wounded look in her eyes as I spoke and it calmed my anger somewhat.

Graham cleared his throat to speak, but she interrupted him. "No, you will not speak on this matter." She spoke quietly, but sternly. "This has nothing to do with you and I'm still your employer and creator."

I stood up and leaned over her desk. "This sure as hell does concern him because he loves me and you sent him away to keep him from me."

She laughed brusquely. "You didn't even care for

him. And now you do? What brings this change of heart?"

"He has been my protector from the moment we met. It just took me a while to realize it."

"He hasn't even told you yet, has he?" She smirked at Graham after she spoke.

"Don't." He glared at her.

"Told me what?"

She laughed. "Ask him, sometime. He has much he hasn't told you, my dear. I only wish I had told you sooner myself and maybe you wouldn't have been so quick to run off with him."

Graham spoke up. "She knows that I love her and she loves me back now. That is all that matters."

Her face twisted when he mentioned that I loved him. "Enough." She stood up and shoved her chair back.

"Guards! Come!" She shouted. She leaned over the desk and whispered to me. "You'll not leave me and live to tell about it."

Graham stepped back quickly and held the door. He wouldn't be able to hold it for long. "I didn't want it to come to this, but if you insist on doing harm to either of us, then I must."

"Speak your piece quickly, then. You haven't got much time." Her face was twisted into a snarl. I looked at them both, afraid and confused.

"Zaleska says that if I turn up dead or missing, she'll speak of what she knows really happened to her father."

The snarl on her face melted away. She stumbled back and sat down. "Guards, stand down for a moment."

Graham let go of the door. "It is something I had suspected for a long time since you'd never spoken of him."

"Stop it. We will not speak of this." She shrieked at Graham. I'd never seen her so unnerved and weak. She looked like the whole world had crumbled all around her.

Meanwhile, a million questions zoomed around my head at the speed of light. What info was he holding over Ilona's head to make such a powerful woman crumble like that? What was Graham keeping from me? How did I get myself into this mess? We obviously had some things to discuss, but for now, he was still my rock and my protector; I clung to him.

Ilona still sat there, looking shaken. I felt some small amount of pity for her.

I rounded the desk and put my arms around her from behind. "I do care for you Ilona. I don't like to see you like this. There has to be a way we can part amicably. We both did this wrong. We hurt each other badly. We both screwed up-"

She gently touched my hands for a second and then pushed me off of her. "Go. Do not come back here to this town or I will hunt you, no matter the consequences. I release both of you."

I grabbed Graham's hand and we walked towards the door. I felt tears sting my eyes and fall onto my cheeks. I looked back once more to witness her beauty. I'd swear there were tears welling up in her eyes too. It was still too raw for me. Even though I loved Graham, part of me would always feel something for her. Despite her cruel nature, I knew she loved me in her own way.

After that, everything happened in a blur. Minutes or hours later, I was at my apartment. I was packing things. Raphe was no longer a worry. We were leaving anyway. In time, he'd forget his obsession with me. Graham and I didn't even speak.

When I was done packing what was important to me, I just sat down on my bed and cried. Graham rubbed my shoulders lovingly. I was bombarded with a harsh variety of thoughts and feelings. I was feeling triumphant and relieved, but I also was sad, angry, hurt, scared, and perplexed by all the things that had been said. Confusion didn't even scratch the surface. I was emotionally exhausted and didn't know which way was up.

Graham finally broke his silence. "Darling, I will run to the store and grab you a coffee. It's been a long night and I can tell you are tired." I nodded. "Need anything else?"

I shook my head and muttered, "Coffee's fine."

I wiped away the tears and went to the bathroom. I washed my face with some cool water. My cheeks were puffy and red. I chuckled at myself for worrying about how I looked at such an odd time. Some time had passed, but I wasn't sure how long it had been since Graham left. I was steadying myself with the edge of the sink and staring into the mirror as the faucet dripped.

I heard the front door open and felt a wave of relief. I smiled. "Darling, I'm so glad you're..." There was someone behind me in seconds and I knew instantly it wasn't Graham, but it was too late. Everything went black.

***

When I came back to the conscious world, I was in Raphe's office, tied to a chair. I had been through so much, I was more tired than scared. My head was throbbing. It took a moment for me to put things together. I didn't think I'd been hit. I assumed they had used chloroform or something like that. I felt that I might vomit.

I was alone in the room so I started trying to scoot

the chair closer to the desk. Surely I could find something to get myself free. I was only two feet from the desk when the door opened. My heart lurched. I stopped my struggling and craned my head to see who was entering.

Raphe's most recent conquest, Akila, was standing there grinning. "Oh, I've been waiting to get you alone for some time. Raphe is busy at the moment and I'm to keep an eye on you until he gets back." She strolled over to me slowly. "How dare you keep toying with Raphe! Let him go. He deserves to be happy."

"Let him go? You've got to be kidding me." I stared at her in disbelief.

She slapped me across the cheek. It left a terrible sting.

"I don't know what he's told you, but I've moved on a long time ago. I want nothing more than to get out of here. You can have him."

She looked confused for a moment. "You're not fooling me, you little slut. You've done nothing but cause him pain and taunt him by sticking around in his life. He could be happy if you'd let him." She grabbed me by the hair. "Your time is almost done. Any second now, he'll be here. And he is very angry. I'll let you think on that. Don't bother trying to escape. I'll be right outside the door and I will be glad for any reason to beat the shit out of you."

She let go of my hair and walked outside. I tried to struggle a little more, but gave up. I was too exhausted to try any further. I resolved myself to let things play out how they would.

Moments ticked by while my mind raced with images of what might happen upon Raphe's arrival. Finally, the door opened and Raphe walked in behind me. He ran his fingers through my hair and I felt a wave of nausea roll through me. He came around and stood over me. "Hello, beautiful."

I glared at him. I didn't have an appropriate response.

"Did you really think you could hide out with your new friends forever? You should have known you couldn't get away from me that easily. You are mine."

The way he said the word mine made my stomach churn.

I felt anger burst out from me. "I am not a possession. I was never yours or anyone else's. I never will be."

He laughed and sat down calmly at his desk. "You are mistaken. I've invested a lot of time, money, and even love on you. You will not run off with a bunch of vampires and leave me holding the bag. I'm the only one who truly cares about you and your career."

I looked at him incredulously. "You paid me a fair wage. But as far as our relationship, you did nothing but cheat on me repeatedly and expect me to just stand by you and take it. You don't care about the advancement of my career. You just don't want me to succeed without you."

He laughed again and sat down at the desk. "Well you can stay tied up like that until you decide you want to give this a try again."

He tried to look like he was doing some work on his computer, but I could tell he was keeping an eye on me.

I smiled slyly. "What about Akila?"

"Akila is fun, but she's not you."

"Why'd you tell her I was trying to get you back?"

"Had to tell her something to justify kidnapping you. I knew bringing you here would upset her, but she means nothing to me. I'll fire her if you just agree to come back, doll." He gave me a charming smile that would have melted me when we were together, but I'd gotten wise since then.

Just then, the door crashed open, and enraged Akila was standing in the doorway. I was thrilled to find she had stuck around and eavesdropped. "You still love her?! You bastard. I can't believe you've been feeding me lies this whole time."

She walked over to me and held me by my hair. "What can I do to this little cunt to make you pay for your sins? Hmmm?"

He jumped up. "Don't you harm a hair on her head or you'll regret it."

He came over and grabbed her by her hair and she let go of mine. He proceeded to start screaming at her and calling her names, but I wasn't paying attention because I felt her slip her hands down behind me and start working on the ropes. I was loose in seconds but I waited for the right moment to escape.

She shoved him back toward the desk and kissed him. I jumped up and ran through the open doorway.

I never even looked back. I just kept running until I got several blocks away. I stopped and hailed a cab.

When I pulled in at my apartment, Graham was outside pacing. I was so relieved to see him. I leaped out of the cab and latched onto Graham. He held me tightly against his body. The cab driver was waiting.

"Can you pay him?"

Graham walked over and slipped the driver some cash.

The second he drove off, Graham grabbed my hands in his and looked at me. "I thought you'd left me."

There was a look of haunted desperation in his eyes that spooked me, but I was so relieved to be with him and feeling safe that I pushed it aside.

I sat for a few minutes to calm myself down. When my heart rate returned to normal, I told Graham what had happened with Raphe. He was overcome with guilt that he wasn't able to protect me. I assured him that now we were safe and it was okay. He was enraged and started ranting about all the things he would do to Raphe, but I put my fingers over his lips.

"No. Let's hurry up and get out of here."

He closed his eyes and buried his face in my hair. "As you wish, my inamorata."

We made a few hasty trips to grab some things and were on our way.

13 THE RUNAWAYS

We headed south this time. I wanted to see Grandma Mae. I needed the comforts only she could provide. Graham was silent. I tried to call Liv, but it went to voicemail. I left her a message telling her that things had been resolved and we were safe but couldn't stay in Maine. I was disappointed that she didn't answer. I hoped she would keep in touch. It felt like I was losing everything at once.

I replayed all that had happened over the past few days in my head. It was complete insanity. My head was a mess. I remembered a time when my life was quite boring. Fear and dread were in the rearview mirror, but confusion was sticking around. I was still glad to have met Graham in spite of everything.

We stopped to rest for the night in a hotel in upstate New York. Even though I was exhausted, I felt as though I'd never fall asleep. Graham held me tightly and even tried to seduce me, but I pushed him away. "Not right now."

He seemed hurt and turned over. He remained quiet.

The longer we lay in bed, the words Ilona had said started to haunt me.

"Graham, what is it you haven't told me?"

"Hmm?"

"What was it Ilona spoke of? That you haven't told me..."

He rolled over and caressed my cheek. He looked in my eyes and underneath the immense love, there was real fear, more fear than I had seen during all the crazy adventures we'd had. Suddenly, I was scared. My heart was thumping loudly in my chest. I couldn't even begin to understand what would cause this fear in him.

"I don't think now is the time..."

"I need to know. Now."

I felt my heartbeat grow faster and louder. He kissed me and sighed. "Ok, but I want you to know that it's all been out of love..."

My heart sank. I knew it was something bad.

He stopped for a moment and sighed.

"Well, let me start from the beginning. After I split from Ilona, I lived in New York for a while. I was living a predatory lifestyle. Lots of sex, blood, and rock n roll." He chuckled at his little joke, nervously. I waited anxiously for him to go on. I started biting my nails.

"Anyway, I was living the lifestyle. You have to realize that vampire lifestyles have only in the past decade or so reformed. I haunted the streets looking for prey almost every night. It's not something I am proud of, but I need you to understand. One night, everything changed for me. While I was wandering on this particular night, I heard the voice of a young girl singing "Somewhere Over the Rainbow" on some side street. The voice was haunting and beautiful. I felt human emotion wash over me like a tidal wave when I heard that voice. It was like the voice was beckoning me..."

Goosebumps formed on my skin. I stopped biting my nails.

"As I grew closer, the voice was even more intoxicating. it was the most beautiful voice I'd ever heard. I followed her and an older lady up the street, at a distance. The older lady stopped to ask someone for directions. The girl played on the sidewalk. I approached cautiously. I bent down upon one knee. This little angel said hello to me."

"Her voice was equally as lovely when not singing. 'What is your name, little one?' I said to her. Her southern accent leaped out at me with all its charm. 'My name is Nina, sir.' I smiled at her. 'That's a lovely name and you are a lovely singer. Keep it up.'"

He paused for a moment to look at me, but I was in shock. I hadn't thought about the trip to New York in years. It was blurry, but now I could see Graham through the fog of memory, looking much the same. Could this be true? It seemed unreal to me that this childhood memory contained Graham. But - I knew. The moment he described the girl singing to me, I knew the story. I'd had a warm feeling about the stranger. I hadn't thought about it in years, but the stranger had stuck like glue to the back of my mind.

He continued. "I was so caught up in following you that I hadn't noticed there had been some thugs following me. There are many anti-vampire groups, especially in larger cities. Well, my lifestyle had attracted their attention. They jumped me while I was focused on you. They dragged me into an alleyway. It happened so fast and I was distracted, so they had a clear advantage." He stared off into space, obviously lost in the memory. "I fought them off for a few minutes but I was outnumbered six to one. I was a vampire, but I had weaknesses just as any man. I managed to bite a chunk out of the neck of one, but they had me held down. I thought to myself 'This is it.'" He swallowed hard and then looked at me as a slight smile curved the edges of his lips.

"But just as I'd given up hope, around the corner ran my little angel with her Grandmother and some policemen. The thugs ran off. The police asked if I was okay and if I wanted to make a statement but I saw my angel walking away and didn't want to waste time with such nonsense. I continued to follow you. I got info on your grandmother and you from the hotel clerk with some bribery. I felt indebted to you. I thought it was a sign that I should change my life. Right then, I swore to protect you. I've checked in on you throughout your life. I've watched you grow up and become a beautiful woman, whom I could not help but fall in love with. I know how strange this all sounds, but I assure you I have never done anything to harm you. I've always kept my distance, no matter how much I wanted to touch you."

"You have to know how creepy this is...To know that you've been following me around for my entire life?" I searched his face. I wasn't sure how to process this information.

He sighed and glanced down with a look of shame. "Yes. I know. That's why I was wary of telling you. But you have to know that it was only with good intentions. I felt an affection for you immediately, but I grew to care about you and your well-being. Please understand this. "

"What part did Ilona play in this?"

"I spoke of you often, but she only had a passing interest until she saw you perform. Then she developed a crush on you, herself."

"...and what other things have you affected in my life?"

"Mostly just kept bullies and jerks away from you. Um, I kind of orchestrated you catching Raphe cheating a few times. I felt you needed to know who he was. He wasn't good for you. I also sent you that brochure with all the lovely pictures of Maine when you were a teen. Wasn't sure it'd do the job, but it did."

"Wow."

The Good, the Bad, the Ugly. I didn't know where to start. The whole thing was just bizarre.

"I'm going to shower."

He lay there, looking dejected.

I cried the whole time I showered. For a while I sat in the bottom of the tub and let the water beat down on me. When I got out, I tip-toed to the bed and he was asleep. I took the hotel stationery into the bathroom and fashioned a letter.

Graham,

I hope you understand that I do still love you, but I need some time to digest what you've told me. I'm going on to my grandmother's. Please do not follow.

Love,
Nina

I slipped out and got the hotel clerk to call a cab to the bus station for me. I felt numb the whole ride down. I don't remember a thing about it. I didn't cry. I didn't think. I simply existed in a coma of misery.

***

Gramma's house helped me come back to life, but I was still miserable without him. Days went by and there was no word from Graham. Part of me wanted that distance, but part of me wanted to know he was nearby to continue being my protector. Gramma knew there was something wrong and she comforted me with food and mindless chatter, but she didn't force me to talk about what was really bothering me.

I called Liv and spilled the beans. I cried my eyes out in the process of explaining the whole story to her.

It was a comfort just to hear her voice. She was very much against Graham after hearing the whole story. I wasn't sure how I felt towards him. I missed him, but I wasn't sure if I missed the love we shared or if it was the sense of safety I missed.

For days, I only existed. I walked around like a zombie. I ignored my problems and immersed myself in television, books, and food with Gramma. I ate enough fried foods to take a few years off my life. Any moment that I didn't distract myself, thoughts of Graham slipped back in, but I didn't want to think about it. I lived in a weird state of numb funk.

On the fourth night, Gramma's card group came over. In all honesty, they were more about gossip than actual card-playing. That night they were playing spades, which was my favorite, but I figured they might hound me about my life and I couldn't handle it, so I hugged them all and excused myself.

I laid in bed to read. I couldn't concentrate. I got up and looked out the window at the stars. I closed my eyes and the tears started to come. It was the first time since the night I'd arrived that I'd really allowed the hurt back in. I wanted him. I didn't care about the past. I knew that he had good intentions. I didn't know how to fix it. I didn't know if I should fix it. I wondered if he was thinking of me too.

Out of the corner of my eye, I saw movement behind the old oak in the backyard. It startled me and I backed away from the window. My heart was doing flips inside my chest.

Just then my phone went off. I grabbed it with unsteady hands. My heart soared to find a text from Graham. "Sing for me?"

I grinned like a fool and ran to the window. I threw it open and belted out Somewhere Over the Rainbow.

He moved out of the shadows and under my window and seemed to bask in the vibrations of my voice.

When I finished the song, I ran downstairs and out the door. Our arms were wrapped around each other. I whispered to him. "Please don't ever lie to me or keep things from me again."

"I promise. Come away with me?" He smiled at me.

"Of course."

As our lips met, I inhaled the sweet smell of my handsome vampire. How could I have thought I didn't need him in my life?

When I came out of my beloved's embrace, there was an applause. The old lady brigade had followed me outside to see what the ruckus was about. We went in with the group and Graham charmed them. They seemed to think he was quite a catch.

I laughed when Gramma leaned over to me and whispered, "He looks familiar." I didn't bother trying to explain it to her.

Graham and I talked things out that night. We stayed up and snuggled in my bed. He shared funny stories about viewing my life from the outside. He said he knew that I was still wary, but he was going to be patient and do everything he could to make it up to me. And I knew that he would.

He shared with me stories about his time with Ilona. We had a new policy of full disclosure. We shared secrets and stories until we passed out from exhaustion.

We stayed another few days at Gramma's. She was unsure about his night hours at first, but I explained that he was in the nightclub business and she accepted that at face value. She, like the other old ladies, had been swept up in his charm.

On our last night there, she took me aside. "Hold on to this one. He's a good one."

I nodded in agreement. "I know. I plan on it."

"Come back to visit soon?"

"I'm sure we will." I wasn't sure if Graham had a plan for where to go or what to do, but I knew he'd allow this if I wanted it. He'd give me whatever my heart desired. I told Gramma goodbye. I grabbed my things and we hit the road.

When we had gone only a few miles, I turned to Graham. "So where are we going, my Inamorata?"

He grinned and squeezed my hand. "It's a surprise."

EPILOGUE

January 19, 2013

"Do you ever miss Ilona?"

Topaz sighed. "Well, I miss not having to live in a fucking van!"

James glared at her. He was a big, muscular vamp with a green mohawk.

Topaz smiled at him. "You know I love you, Jimbo. You're my maker. Ilona was good to me for a while, but then she threw me away like I was a piece of trash for some slutty redhead. I don't want to talk about it."

"Are you ever getting the band back together?"

"I'd like to, but they aren't exactly supportive of my decision to become a vamp. They say I make them nervous. I guess they have a point."

"I know you miss it. Maybe you could start a new band with vamps or some vamp-friendly humans? You should think about it."

She rolled her eyes.

"I'm serious!"

She leaned over to the driver's seat and kissed him gently on the cheek. "I'll consider it when I'm done having fun. Right now, all I can think about is dinner!"

He jumped out of the van and opened the passenger side door for Topaz with a gentlemanly flourish. "After you, love. This one looks delicious."

Topaz grinned at a girl alone on the sidewalk. The girl looked to be in her late teens and was talking animatedly on her cell phone while pacing the sidewalk.

Topaz turned to James. "It's 2 a.m. Do her parents know where she is?"

James snickered.

They were on her before she knew what had happened. She didn't even scream.